BEWARE THE HEARTMAN

BEWARE THE HEARTMAN

SHAKIRAH BOURNE

Scholastic Press / New York

Library of Congress Cataloging-in-Publication Data available

ISBN 978-1-338-78359-9

10 9 8 7 6 5 4 3 2 1   24 25 26 27 28

Printed in the USA   61

First edition, September 2024

Book design by Stephanie Yang

To all the readers who asked for more.

CHAPTER 1

The smell of sweaty armpits and purple Kool-Aid breath whacks me in the face. Ah, the taste of victory!

My teammates pile on top of me, and I can't decide whether to cheer or hold my breath.

It's the quarterfinals of the Barbados Youth Cricket competition, and I've just annihilated the last player with my fastball, taking my team into the semifinal for the first time in years. Hands pull me from the tangle of arms and legs and lift me to the sky.

I inhale fresh air and then crane my neck toward the stands, checking for Daddy; he never misses a match. Sure enough, he's there in the middle row roaring his approval. He pumps his fists and almost knocks out the man selling nut cakes nearby. Thankfully, Miss Alleyne, my teacher and Daddy's new girlfriend, uses her wicked fast reflexes to stop the man from toppling over.

I search for Ahkai, my neighbor and best friend, but judging from the lack of "whoop whoop" in the crowd, he didn't make it.

Again.

This is the third game in a row he's missed. Ahkai doesn't like large crowds. Actually, he doesn't like small groups of people either. He's on the autism spectrum and mainly talks to me and his mom, Miss Mo. Everyone else gets a blank stare, or if he likes you, a small nod and smile.

Still, Ahkai attends my cricket matches to support me, and though he spends most of the game reading, he pays attention whenever I have the ball and cheers at the end of every game.

I brush away the twinge of disappointment and try to focus on the celebration.

"Okay, okay, that's enough!"

Jared, the team captain, helps me to my feet with one hand. He's really strong, and the only person on the team who is taller than me. And he thinks he's a comedian too. Off the field, he cracks the corniest jokes and then laughs at his own punch lines. I guess some of them are funny.

Okay, I admit, all of them are funny. Not that I'd ever let him know.

"Good work, everyone," Jared manages, before giving in to another sneeze attack.

My smile fades as I spot the cotton fibers dancing in the air.

The silk cotton tree nearby is shedding. Poor Jared had an allergic reaction so strong, he had to drop out of the game.

We head to the pavilion, still waving to our supporters in the stands. Casper, our eccentric school grounds-keeper, is racing around the field with a giant yellow foam hand. He uses it to scratch his armpits while a man—most likely the person he stole it from—chases after him.

Coach Broomes waits by the benches with his clip-board in hand and his mouth pressed into a thin line as he stares at Jared with concern. Hopefully Jared won't sneeze again, or else Coach may call for an ambulance.

"Good game; you made me proud. Two more wins and that trophy is ours."

While the team chants "Fairy Vale!" Coach Broomes bends to speak into my ear. "Miss Cadogan, the match officials named you Man of the Match, but um, well, I ain' too sure how, well, you tell me what to do."

Coach Broomes is still getting accustomed to having a girl cricketer on the team. Miss Alleyne made him do sensitivity training after she overheard him asking if I would need a jockstrap.

"Player of the Match is fine." I try to contain my excitement, but I want to break into song and dance. It's my first award!

After the presentation ceremony, I rush to Daddy and leap into his outstretched arms. Cricket is more than a game for us; it's also one of the few connections we have to my mum. Whenever I hit the stumps or catch a ball to get a batsman out, I feel her spirit cheering with Daddy in the stands.

"Let's go," Dad says, still beaming at me. "Miss Mo invite we over for roast breadfruit this evening."

My mouth waters at the future taste of delicious roasted breadfruit slathered in Mello-Kreem butter and ketchup. Ahkai probably had to help his mother clean and bone fish for dinner. Yes, that's why he didn't show up to the game. The thought cheers me up.

I knew Ahkai wouldn't abandon me without a good reason.

Miss Mo only asked me, Daddy, Miss Alleyne, and a few of her family members to dinner, but when the smell of roast breadfruit hits the air, neighbors show up with hungry smiles, or as Miss Mo says, "With nothing but their two long arms swinging."

This is how it is in Fairy Vale. Breadfruit-smoke signals an invite to the whole community, but I guess that's what happens when you choose to eat outdoors for the whole world to see.

When we arrive, the circle of large rocks and wood is already ablaze, with about a dozen large breadfruits in the fire. People sit around on plastic crates and bricks, sharing drinks and every so often glancing at the breadfruits to guess when they'll be ready. Miss Mo gives us plastic plates from the large stack in her hands.

"Where's Ahkai?" I ask, looking around for him. He normally occupies a space away from people.

"Out in the backyard," Miss Mo replies. "Tell him come for food before everything gone. Hallam, the garbage right there!" She yells at a little boy who threw his cup on the grass. "Pick it up! You born behind a cow backside or what?"

I leave her quarreling with the litterbug and enter the house. From the hallway, I see Ahkai perched on the step, whittling away at some new masterpiece. He's a genius when it comes to woodwork and gifted me a pendant with a hummingbird in mid-flight, a symbol of when we first met and our friendship. I hurry over, excited to tell him about my cricket victory, but then I come to a dead stop.

Ahkai is sitting next to a girl, close enough for their arms to touch if they wanted to.

It's a warm night, yet the girl is wearing a black long-sleeved dress with a large sailor collar shaped like two napkins on her shoulders. Her long, straight jet-black hair is in a braid laced with a light-blue ribbon.

I've never seen her before, but I feel a powerful wave of dislike. My body goes into fight mode; she has to be keeping Ahkai on the step by force. He never lets anyone so close; only me and Miss Mo are allowed in his personal space.

I haven't made a sound, but the girl stiffens, cocks her head, and turns to me. Our eyes lock, and our stares play a game of tug-of-war.

She furrows her thin, almost nonexistent, eyebrows. She seems upset that I interrupted her alone time with *my* best friend. There's nothing loving about her heart-shaped face. Her skin is a few shades lighter than my dark brown complexion, and as I get closer, I notice brown freckles splattered across her cheeks.

"Who are you?" I demand as soon as I sit next to Ahkai.

"Human?" She speaks in a falling tone, as if the words

dropped off a cliff. It is very, very, very irritating.

Ahkai, as always, notices the tension but pretends that he doesn't. "This is Lynne." He pauses. "A family friend from overseas. She's staying with my cousin Ramona."

I'm taken aback for a second because not only did Ahkai speak in Lynne's presence, but he also did it in his regular voice too. Not a mumble or whisper. He rarely talks out loud, especially around people he doesn't trust or feel comfortable with. Even Daddy and Miss Alleyne have gotten only a couple of sentences out of him. Who is this "family friend" that's privileged enough to get three lines in a row? Now I'm even more curious about her, and most important, when she'll be gone.

"So, when are you returning *overseas*?" I ask her.

"When I'm ready." She plucks a pebble from the soil and adds it to a pile of oddly shaped rocks at her feet.

Talking to her is like pulling teeth.

Ahkai leans over and whispers in my ear, "I like her. Be nice."

Where's that whittling knife? His words stabbed me in the heart. My Ahkai, would-fake-a-coma-to-avoid-people Ahkai, *likes* someone. Is this why he missed my cricket match? Because he found someone he likes more than me? I can't deal with this. Not now. Not ever.

I jump to my feet. "Miss Mo says it's time to eat." I

pass him a plate, and then, because I'm supposed to *be nice*, I shove one at Lynne as well.

She holds the plate with two fingers as if it's dirty. "Plastic is terrible for the environment. Doesn't Miss Mo have real plates?"

This girl thinks she's too good for disposables. I do a mock bow. "Forgive me for displeasing you with our flimsy wares, Your Majesty." Then I whisper to Ahkai, "Is she a Queen Mary student?"

Ahkai and I took the dreaded Common Entrance Exam weeks ago and we both believe we did well enough to get into Lamming Secondary, the top school in Barbados. It's definitely my first choice. But Queen Mary is the first choice for posh, rich kids. I've heard that the students sip soda in fancy teacups and eat cucumber sandwiches for lunch with a knife and fork.

Lynne would fit right in.

"Lynne is waiting for the Common Entrance Exam results too," Ahkai replies, before stepping inside.

"I'm just saying, there are a bunch of ceramic plates in the cupboard," Lynne grumbles behind me.

A slow smile spreads across my face. "That is a good idea. You should get one. Go ahead, I dare you."

Then I can sit back and watch Miss Mo explode when she sees Lynne with one of her "good plates" outdoors.

I shouldn't have looked so eager. Lynne cocks her head in suspicion and decides to keep her toxic plastic plate.

When we get our food, I deliberately choose a spot on the grass with enough space for two people, but Lynne squeezes next to Ahkai, forcing me into Miss Mo's bushes. She smirks at me and then digs into her giant heap of breadfruit covered with margarine-ketchup sauce and tuna.

I do not like her.

I do not like her at all.

I slap a small branch away from my face, and something clunks me on the head. "Ow!"

Ahkai, who had been picking smoky, burnt flecks off his breadfruit, takes up the ripe pomegranate that fell from the tree.

"Dessert. Thank you, Jo." He breaks the fruit in half and puts a piece on my plate.

I glare at him for a few seconds, but when his mouth starts to twitch, a laugh sneaks out of me. I can never stay mad at him for long, and in this sort of setting, with a crackling fire and delicious food, the laughter becomes contagious and spreads around the garden.

The adults exchange stories from when they were growing up, and Miss Alleyne has everyone in stitches with her cadet boot camp tales, sharing how she accidentally ambushed her drill sergeant taking a pee in a gully.

But everything goes downhill when Ahkai's cousin Ramona and her husband get ready to leave.

"Make sure to take off your shoes and walk backward into yuh house so no evil spirits can follow you inside," Miss Mo calls after them.

Ramona laughs. "Thank you, Auntie, now lemme get home before the Heartman catch me."

"Heartman? What is a Heartman?" Lynne asks.

I groan, knowing what's coming next. It was unlikely to get through a night by the fire without Miss Mo telling stories about some terrifying folklore creature, but why did Ramona have to bring up the scariest of them all? I went to bed with the lights on the first time I heard about the legendary Heartman, and after my experience last year, I don't even want to *think* about the possibility of him being real too. Every kid on the island has whispered his name in fear at least once. Lynne is from "overseas" so she can hear his name without feeling that twinge of terror.

Miss Mo is not one to pass up an opportunity to scare an innocent kid. She clears her throat and draws close to the fire, her shadow looming in the trees. Everyone grows quiet, waiting for her performance.

"Lynne, you don't want to ever come face-to-face with the Heartman. He's an evil, evil man who made a pact with the devil and now has to pay off the debt with hearts . . . and he like children's organs the most. He does prowl the street in a hearse, searching for hard-ears children who stay out after dark. And if he catch you, he will rip yuh heart right out yuh chest."

Lynne's expression grows more and more cross, but Miss Mo isn't discouraged. She flings her hands in the air.

"He wears a black musty cloak, crawling with centi-pedes. People say his face so evil, even demons cover their eyes, breath so stink it could give you a sore throat. He so ugly . . ."

Miss Mo goes on and on, her descriptions getting wilder and wilder, desperate for some reaction from Lynne.

Finally, Lynne scoffs. "Y'all made this up to scare kids into getting home on time. None of this is real." Lynne looks to Ahkai for support, but he keeps his head down.

"He was based off a real serial killer," he mumbles.

That's what makes the Heartman so terrifying—he was an actual person. People who choose to turn them-selves into monsters are the scariest.

"The Heartman stories started in the 1950s and

1960s." Miss Alleyne speaks up, bringing fact to the lore. "There was a serial killer on the loose, used to leave the bodies of his victims in the cane fields."

Suddenly, the disturbing story turns into something much more sinister. I signed up for a simple breadfruit meal, not a serving of body horror. I try to block out the conversation; think about cricket, pancakes, and everything good; but it doesn't work. My ears disobey me; I'm scared, but curious too.

"I remember those days," says Aunt Jackie. She's one of those old women who sits on their porches all day and glares at kids and then complains about how unmannerly we are. "So much murder. Started when the Heartman killed that child just like that. *Pax!*"

We all jump, even Lynne, when Aunt Jackie slashes a hand in the air and slaps it down onto her other palm. Ahkai whispers "pax" four more times under his breath.

"Then he drain all the blood and cut out the heart, left the rest in the cane fields for us to find. Up north, we ain' had no proper lighting back then—dark, lonely roads. Nobody ain' dare leave the house by themselves, and we use to rush to get home before nightfall. And remember Goodman?"

A chorus of low murmurs fills the air, hushed whispers of

"can't forget 'bout he" and "we don't talk about Goodman." And so, they immediately talked about Goodman. He was a man who disappeared from the village, and his case remains unsolved to this day.

"And you know, Casper says the Heartman kidnapped his wife," someone adds.

But this time, they all laugh. Everyone except, me, Daddy, and Ahkai. I used to laugh at Casper's stories too, until I had my own encounter with the supernatural. Now I don't think he's as mad as everyone believes. And I know Daddy and Ahkai feel the same way.

"He should be in a madhouse, not working at a school," says one of the men who spends his whole day at the rum shop.

Finally, we leave Miss Mo's, the sound of laughter fading behind us as we cross the street, and I grow tense again. *The Heartman isn't real*, I tell myself. *They're all just stories.* But my mind doesn't fully believe it. So instead, I focus on brighter thoughts. *It's going to be okay. You and Ahkai will soon be at Lamming school together. Lynne won't be in Fairy Vale for much longer.*

Then, something rustles in the hibiscus bushes underneath the kitchen window. It's too dark to see more than shadows, even with the half-moon bright in the sky, and the bush is thick enough to hide a human . . . or something not human. My breath catches in my throat and only returns when a lizard scurries across the branch.

I'm becoming way too paranoid.

"Bean? Everything all right?" Daddy is waiting for me in the doorway.

I force a smile on my face. "Yup."

I amble into the house, pretending I didn't expect to be attacked on my front step, but I can't hold back the sigh of relief when Daddy bolts the door.

CHAPTER 2

Miss Alleyne normally leaves on Sunday nights, so I'm surprised to see her in the kitchen the next morning, transformed into teacher mode—that's when she has her bleached locs in a tight bun instead of hanging loose around her shoulders.

"Mornin', Bean," Daddy says, putting a plate with fried eggs and plantain on the table. He glances nervously at me, waiting for my reaction.

I make a great show of rubbing my eyes and blinking, as if Miss Alleyne is a mirage. She watches with an amused smirk.

"Interesting," I say, drawing out the word.

Dad makes himself busy wiping down the counter,

even though it's sparkling clean. I wink at Miss Alleyne, and the two of us burst out laughing.

Who'd have thought I'd be happy my teacher is dating my Dad? At first it was sooooo awkward, as if school followed me home on weekends. But in a short time, Miss Alleyne has become someone I'd be terrified to lose.

"What I miss?" Dad's bemused expression makes us laugh even harder.

He can be a little oblivious, but I understand why he's worried. I reacted badly when he started dating again, playing pranks on all his dates to scare them away. I'm pretty sure there is a Josephine Cadogan support group somewhere . . .

No one can replace my mum. But Miss Alleyne eased into a space in my heart I didn't know existed. And before, there was sometimes a twinge of sadness behind Daddy's smiles. Now they're full of light.

"Think wunna smart? Aite, keep it up, keep it up," Dad says, shaking his head. "I planning to fish up north today, so see if Miss Mo can take you and Ahkai to school."

I groan. "Ma'am, I'm letting you know now, we're going to be late."

Miss Alleyne is forever trying to get me to call her Aurora, but that's too weird. She'll always be Miss Alleyne or ma'am to me.

"I could ask Miss Price to make room for you," Miss Alleyne offers.

A delicious piece of greasy plantain falls from my mouth. Go to school in a car with a bunch of *teachers*?! I'd rather arrive at the gate in a rusty wheelbarrow. But how can I refuse without hurting Miss Alleyne's feelings?

"Kidding!" she says.

Now she and Daddy are laughing at me.

I sag with relief. "Good one."

After breakfast, I head over to Ahkai's house, swinging my empty backpack around my finger. It's the last week of school before the summer break, but there hasn't been much to do since we took the Common Entrance Exam.

I swing open the kitchen door and automatically bend down to pick up the key that always falls from the lock. Miss Mo keeps keys in the keyholes to stop soucouyants—vampire-like creatures who shed their skin and turn into a ball of fire—from slipping inside the house. It doesn't make sense to me, since the louvers are open at night for the breeze. Can't soucouyants simply fly through the front windows? Unless they're afraid of her flower-print curtains.

Miss Mo, as usual, is on the phone, propped against the wall by the stove, but I'm not prepared to see Lynne at the kitchen table, in a black nightgown with a lace ruffled collar, gobbling down a mountain of eggs and hot dogs.

I point a finger. "What are *you* doing here?"

Lynne raises a mocking eyebrow but continues to eat her breakfast for three.

"Wait, hol' on, hol' on, Marva." Miss Mo glares at me.

"Good morning, Miss Mo," I say quickly before she can scold me. Nothing matters more in Miss Mo's household than manners and Jesus.

Miss Mo narrows her eyes but thankfully lets my slip pass. "Ramona overwhelmed with the new babies, so I told her Lynne could stay here for the time being," she says, and then puts the phone back to her ear. "Five babies, you could believe it? God bless she real good. We gotta plan a fundraiser to help with expenses."

"Staying here?! For how long?"

"'Til whenever, we do for family," Miss Mo replies, and then to Marva. "Remember we going up River Bay on Saturday. No no. Clyde ain' coming, remember he dead last year?"

I can't believe I have to see Lynne's condescending face whenever I come over. Lynne, who still hasn't said a word, takes a plastic carton of milk from the counter and puts it in a green recycling bin that is new to the kitchen.

She must have brought the bin with her luggage. No one in Fairy Vale recycles. Then Miss Mo throws a plastic egg crate into the bin as well, as if it is routine.

Grrrr.

I need to clear my head so I can come up with an operation to get rid of this nuisance family friend. "Miss Mo, Daddy asked if you could take me and Ahkai to school today."

"Sorry, Jo, I have to drop Lynne at Saint Williams this morning," she replies, and then to Marva. "That's the private primary school outside of the village." Then back to me. "You and Ahkai can walk or take the bus. Why you letting in all the flies?"

I close the door and start to head upstairs to complain to Ahkai. I don't live here, but I spend more time at Miss Mo's than my own house. I should have been consulted about Lynne's stay.

Then Ahkai enters the kitchen with an unusually big smile, so big that his dimples almost touch his glasses. But I'm distracted by the darkness in his hands. It unfurls and creeps up his arms, and suddenly, a glassy eyeball with a dash of yellow peers up at me.

"Everyone, this is Inkblot. My new cat." Ahkai holds it up in the air. "He is beautiful. I found him in the garden."

There is silence for a few seconds.

"Marva, lemme call you back," says Miss Mo.

Inkblot paws at the cat-shaped pendant around Ahkai's neck. He had made it to honor his old cat, Simba. But unlike Simba, who was a sweet tabby who liked to cuddle, this cat looks as if it would bite off your fingers if you tried to scratch its ears.

"Ahkai, black cats are bad luck! The devil's pets!" Miss Mo grasps her own necklace—a holy cross encrusted in crystal. Ahkai and Inkblot stare at her with identical expressions of annoyance.

I don't think there's anything dangerous about a cat, but I never thought a snake could pop out of a comb either, and it happened. It's best to be on the safe side. We can't afford any more bad luck, not after what we barely survived.

"Well, now he's mine," Ahkai replies. He grabs a can of tuna from the cupboard, and Inkblot meows five times, like he knows it's Ahkai's favorite number. The cat fits right into the household, just like Lynne. I switch my gaze between Lynne in her nightie and the furry cat—they must have the same stylist.

"I don't know about this, Ahkai." I grimace when I'm on the receiving end of his dirty side-eye.

Lynne gives me a sly look. "I think you're scared of a little cat. You think it has powers? That it'll sneak into your room and strangle you with its magical whiskers? Go on, touch him. I dare you."

"Nobody cares what you think!" I snap at her. If she knew that some folklore creatures were real, she'd have more respect for superstition.

"Well, I also think he's cute," Lynne says with an attitude. She bends down to stroke Inkblot's head. Unfortunately, the cat doesn't maul her hand like it does the can of tuna. I get even more irritated when Ahkai shoots Lynne a grateful smile. How can I discourage him from keeping the cat now?

Lynne goes upstairs to get ready for school, and I inch over to Miss Mo.

"Do something," I hiss under my breath, but she seems reluctant, even though she was preaching about the cat's demonic origins a minute ago.

Ahkai was devastated after Simba's disappearance last year. Miss Mo probably doesn't want him to go through that loss again.

Miss Mo gives me a "What can I do?" look, as if she doesn't own the house. "Best to keep Inkblot in the backyard for now so he doesn't get away."

The dreaded cat finishes the tuna, and Ahkai lifts him into his arms. I follow them into the backyard.

"What is it with you and stray animals?" He ignores me, so I try to appeal to his rational side. "This could be someone else's cat."

He pauses but then shrugs. "I have not seen any missing cat flyers."

I let out a breath of exasperation.

The cat races over to the outdoor sink. He leaps into the air, trying to claw at some wasps above the faucet. Then, the black cat stops.

In. Mid. Air.

Its four legs dangle above the sink, knocking away one of the plastic bottles I use to practice my bowling.

I check to see if Ahkai is seeing a floating cat too, but he's busy dusting cat hair from his school pants. When I glance back at Inkblot, he is on the ground, licking his paws. He returns my stare, flops onto his belly, and stretches.

I shake my head to clear it. I can't allow Lynne to mess with my brain. A floating cat . . . she would have a field day with that one.

Then, a strangled squawk comes from inside the house.

Moments later, Miss Mo appears at the door, clutching the top of her flower-print house dress.

"My friend's sister's cousin's next-door neighbor who works at the Ministry just call! Wunna getting back the exam results today!"

CHAPTER 3

Miss Mo's little Toyota Starlet trudges up Coconut Hill, toward the giant silk cotton tree, its muscular branches blocking the sun.

I used to sit under that shade, staring out at the glimmering sea and inhaling the salty smell of the ocean. It was my sanctuary, but now I avoid the area whenever possible, choosing to take the much longer way to and from school.

It's been ten months since I cut into the tree and accidentally released Mariss, a spiteful half-woman, half-snake sea spirit. I try to carry on with life, choosing to forget that Mariss kidnapped Daddy and then commanded the ocean to swallow me whole. A strong wind rattles through the leaves and I crank up the window, pretending to shiver from the cold.

She is gone. Life goes on.

The entrance to Mariss's cave, the rock shaped like a fist in the ocean, had mysteriously disappeared months ago. People blamed the phenomenon on climate change, but I took it as a good sign—Mariss was truly out of our lives.

Nothing so awful could possibly happen again.

Cars line the road as we get near to Fairy Vale Academy, double-parked and creating traffic. Of course, everyone knows someone who knows someone who works at the Ministry of Education. Parents stand outside the school under umbrellas, waiting to hear the exam results.

All this time I've been so confident about my exam performance, but suddenly I have the urge to vomit. Ahkai had remembered most of the math and English exam questions and quizzed me on the answers afterward. I'm pretty sure I did well enough to make it into the top school, but there's still a chance that I didn't. That Ahkai and I may be going to different schools. That we would be separated and left to deal with strange environments and new people all by ourselves.

I take a deep breath and focus on something satisfying, like Lynne's scowling face when Miss Mo dumped her at a bus stop; she didn't want to miss hearing Ahkai's results.

Ahkai and I leave Miss Mo blaring her horn and follow the procession of kids through the school gate, while strangers yell encouraging words at us. Daddy is probably out at sea, unaware of this pandemonium. I glance at Ahkai, worried he'd be triggered by the chaos. He still has his blank expression, but then, he hooks his pinkie into mine.

I have to get into Lamming Secondary with him, I just *have* to.

Casper is in the middle of the road, directing traffic with the giant foam finger. He believes he's a narrator on a wildlife TV show and villagers are members of the animal kingdom. "Today a herd of massive wildebeests canter in panic, leaving a path of destruction in their wake!" he cries.

We wait in the classroom together with the other students, who debate which person got the highest marks and who most likely failed. *Where is Miss Alleyne?* My stomach is heavy, like I swallowed a giant rock. I need her now; she has this sensei sixth sense to say the right things, and also knows when words aren't needed at all.

The classroom door opens, and I perk up in my seat, desperate to see her reassuring, smiling face.

But it's not Miss Alleyne.

"Mr. Atkins?" I whisper in surprise.

I haven't seen my old form teacher since Miss Alleyne substituted for him last year, when he took leave to travel.

Mr. Atkins looks exactly the same, down to the brown, stiff shirt-jacs he fancies, the ones with four pockets and embroidered pleats at the sides, and plain brown slacks. Put him against a whiteboard and he'd resemble a thin roti on a plate. Not that I would ever say that out loud. Mr. Atkins is an ex-soldier, and I've never seen him laugh. Not once. The closest thing to a smile on his face is his thick handlebar mustache.

He is a slight man, but he radiates authority—you can tell he's capable of disarming someone with only his little finger. He can calm a noisy classroom by just raising an eyebrow. Even now, though he hasn't said a word, all the students are on their feet, waiting for his instructions.

"Everyone in alphabetical order now," he commands, in his firm, soft voice.

"Quietly," he adds, when we hit into tables and chairs to find our places.

"Now proceed to the hall."

"We're getting the results in front of the whole school?!" I exclaim.

Mr. Atkins frowns at me. "Cadogan, do not speak unless spoken to. Though I shouldn't be surprised at your lack of manners."

I am shocked. Mr. Atkins was always super strict, but he was never mean to me.

"And your uniform is supposed to be two inches longer. What is this unladylike behavior?"

Heat rushes to my face. I glance around at my classmates. Many other girls have skirts falling just above their knees instead of below them, so why is he picking on me? The boys are wearing dark blue shorts; it doesn't matter that their ashy knees are exposed for the world to see. At least I rub cocoa butter on mine.

Mr. Atkins isn't finished. "Clearly, you have no respect for rules. What's this I hear about you being on a boy's cricket team?"

"That's quite enough." Miss Alleyne steps inside the classroom, and I swear, the entire class exhales in relief.

"Aurora, I thought you'd switched schools by now."

Mr. Atkins's eyes rove disapprovingly over her attire.

She wore her bright sunflower dress today. *Gasp, you can see her knees! Oh, the horror.*

"I know you get"—Mr. Atkins pauses—"restless."

Miss Alleyne grinds her teeth. "That's Miss Alleyne, Mr. Atkins. And you know Fairy Vale hired me full-time. I believe you're supposed to be somewhere else now, sir."

They glare at each other while the class looks on in amazement. I've never seen Miss Alleyne so close to losing her temper before. It seems like neither of them will back down, but then Mr. Atkins turns away. His eyes shoot daggers in my direction before he leaves the classroom.

Miss Alleyne takes a deep breath and then plasters a smile on her face. "Everyone ready?"

And just like that, my stomach drops to the floor. Miss Alleyne takes one look at my face and then puts Ahkai in front of me, though he should be farther back with the rest of the M's.

It helps.

Just before we get to the hall, as we're passing through a dark corridor, Miss Alleyne pulls me into her arms and gives me the hug I needed.

See? No. Words. Necessary.

"Do you have to leave Fairy Vale now that Mr. Atkins is back?" I hold my breath as I wait for her answer.

Miss Alleyne squeezes me tighter. "I'm not going anywhere. You're stuck with me."

I release my breath and pretend that I wasn't nervous.

In the hall, Principal Clarke, an unsmiling lady who we usually only see for major announcements and punishments, goes to the mic onstage and clears her throat. "Good morning, students. In my hand, I have the results of this year's Common Entrance Exam. Now, I would like to remind you that all secondary schools are equal, and there is no such thing as a bad school."

Quiet snickers ripple through the assembly. Everyone knows that's a lie. If it were true, parents would celebrate when their kids passed to any school, not just a select few.

Principal Clarke clears her throat again. "And now, I'm pleased to announce the top student of Fairy Vale Academy of Excellence, who not only is the top student in the school but on the entire island. With one hundred percent in math, ninety-nine percent in English, and an A on their essay, Ahkai Moses will be going to Lamming Secondary!"

There's a roar of applause. I squeal and hug Ahkai first, and then everyone else joins in. Ahkai is completely flabbergasted. We hear cheers from the parents outside, and then a high scream of "thank you, Jesus!" from someone who could only be Miss Mo.

Ahkai recovers from his shock and starts to shy away from other people's embraces. Like me, he's never been good at making friends. I shiver at the thought of us going to different schools. If I can barely connect with people who share my passion for cricket, it will be even worse for Ahkai.

Ahkai finally makes it onto the stage and has a photo shoot with Principal Clarke and several news reporters. Soon, my happiness drains into fear. The kids around me fidget and bite their fingernails. We all wait for the principal to read the rest of the results. To get into Lamming Secondary, I need at least 90 percent in math and English, and an A on my essay.

Ahkai soon gets tired of the picture taking. He loses his smile, and his frantic eyes find mine. I give him a thumbs-up, and he nods and puts on a blank, bored expression. I close my eyes and plead to the universe. Ahkai and I need each another; I have to get into Lamming.

Finally, Principal Clarke starts to read the rest of the results in alphabetical order. The atmosphere in the hall grows tense, only breaking for scattered applause when a student passes to a top school.

All schools are equal, my foot.

I wipe my sweaty hands on my uniform. At least in a few months I'll no longer have to wear Fairy Vale Academy's ugly blue-and-pink tunics, though Lamming's uniform isn't that much better to be honest. Their green-and-white tunics still have these awful pleats.

"Josephine Cadogan."

I sway when Principal Clarke calls my name. A solid figure presses against my back, providing support. The waft of vanilla tells me it's Miss Alleyne, and I lean against her in relief.

"You have scored ninety-one percent in math, ninety percent in English, and an A on your essay!"

Principal Clarke seems surprised at my high grades. I'm too overjoyed to care. With those marks I should make it into Lamming. *I did it!* Ahkai starts to shake on the stage in excitement.

"Congratulations!" Principal Clarke continues. "You have passed to Queen Mary College!"

CHAPTER 4

I immediately burst into tears after Principal Clarke ruined my life.

I dash from the hall before anyone can stop me, heading toward the silk cotton tree, until I remember that it's not my safe space anymore. I whirl around and race to the tamarind tree near the cricket field instead.

How could fate be so cruel to separate me and Ahkai? And worse, force me into a place where I do not belong. Imagine Daddy's old jeep, Jalopy, with its rusty doors and dented bumper, parked next to shiny limousines and luxury vehicles. I will never fit in with the rich kids at Queen Mary, who would turn their noses up at me, as if they could smell the poor on my uniform. I sit under the tree and put my head on my knees and sob until I run out of tears.

It's not long before I feel a presence next to me. I know it's Ahkai. Some other person would ask something silly, like "Are you okay?" even though it's clear I'm not.

Ahkai waits until I am ready to talk.

I lift my head and wipe my eyes with the back of my hand. "I really tried, you know."

"Queen Mary is a good school," Ahkai replies, twisting his cat pendant.

"Lamming is better."

"Actually, I read that thirty-seven percent of educators believe Lamming is much better in academics whereas Queen Mary—"

"It's better because *you* will be there." I turn away to hide my face, tears coming to my eyes again. I guess I still have more inside. My emotions can be so humiliating. Sometimes I wish I could go back to the time when I couldn't cry.

Ahkai taps me on my shoulder. "I have a solution."

"We can't run away. We don't have money for food."

"You do not need money to request a school transfer."

Ahkai fills me in on the process. Daddy could fill out a form to request a school transfer from the Ministry of

Education. The deadline to submit the form is in three weeks. A little ray of hope blossoms inside my chest. All is not lost. I can still fix this.

"Time to go back to class," he says, tugging my foot.

I expect Miss Alleyne to be waiting for me by the classroom door, but by now everyone knows their fate, and she's at the back of the classroom comforting a sobbing girl with large brown ribbons in her hair.

"She failed," Ahkai whispers to me, and shame immediately floods through me. Here I am throwing a tantrum because I passed to a top school, when others are much worse off than me. Plus, it should be easy to transfer to Lamming with my high grades.

I sit quietly at my desk and bounce my cricket ball in my hands, trying to ignore the many classmates who, after years of being in the same class as Ahkai, suddenly have the urge to talk to him today. He mostly nods and smiles, and glances at me nervously while they make conversation around him. I'm desperate for school to end so that I can talk to Daddy about the transfer to Lamming.

Miss Alleyne surprises the class with fried chicken and pizza from Chefette. Just when I think she can't outdo herself, she winks at me and slips a crispy apple pie onto my desk—my favorite! Some of my anxiety fades away, and the delicious greasy food helps the hours to slip by faster.

On the way home, I fidget in the back seat as Miss Mo stops to tell every pedestrian about Ahkai's achievement. By the time we turn into the street, I'm practically bouncing in the seat. We finally *finally* pull up to Miss Mo's house, but Daddy's not home! I get out the car, and, instead of heading inside, I wait impatiently on the curb, hoping to see Jalopy in the distance. I'm still outside when Miss Mo's screech pierces the air.

I scramble toward her cry, expecting the worse, but even though I've dealt with snake monsters and lionfish with a taste for humans, nothing prepares me for what I encounter in the kitchen.

Lynne is hugging Ahkai—and he's not pulling away.

And then it gets worse.

"Lynne passed to Lamming school too!" Miss Mo yells. She's so excited she can't figure out who to call first. She punches several numbers into the phone, disconnecting each time, until she gives up and starts to sing a gospel song.

No one notices that I'm still by the door, not joining in with the celebrations. Or that my cricket ball fell to the ground, along with my heart.

I observe Lynne and Ahkai, still in their embrace,

and imagine the future: Lynne and Ahkai walking into Lamming, hand in hand. Lynne and Ahkai sitting next to each other in class. Lynne and Ahkai laughing at an inside joke.

At a previous cricket match, one of the substitute boys spoke about how his friend deserted him when he moved on to Queen Mary school. Is the same thing going to happen to me and Ahkai? Will we become polite strangers who nod at each other in passing cars?

No.

I won't allow it.

Jalopy's loud engine pulls into our driveway in the nick of time, preventing my meltdown. I race across the street, not even sparing the two seconds to check for oncoming traffic.

Daddy notices me as soon as he steps out of Jalopy and greets me with a big smile and open arms. "Queen Mary!"

I stop before he can pull me into his arms, bending over to catch my breath.

"No no, I have to go to Lamming, with Ahkai— Lamming, not Queen Mary, I hate Queen Mary," I manage to tell him in between breaths.

The smile slides off Daddy's face, and I grab both of his hands. "We can fix this, Daddy! We can get a school transfer. It's easy, we just have to fill out the form."

But to my horror, Daddy doesn't nod and reassure me that we're totally going to rectify this horrid mistake. He isn't keen on the idea. I can tell from the strained, pitiful expression on his face. It's the same one he has whenever we can't afford something, like in the moment he's wondering what could have been if he had made different choices.

"Bean, I sorry but—"

I'm going to lose my friend.

I dash upstairs to my room before Daddy can finish his sentence.

But I'm not ready to give up hope yet. Daddy's a simple man who doesn't like stressful situations. He just needs more time to process everything and to understand how much I want to go to school at Lamming.

I can't leave Ahkai alone, or worse, with Lynne.

CHAPTER 5

The next day, I pretend to be sick to avoid talking to anyone.

"Bean, yuh can't hide 'way forever," Daddy says, hovering over my bed.

I squeeze my eyes shut even tighter. He sighs but lets me stay home from school.

I don't want to move from under my sheets, but later in the afternoon, I remember about cricket practice. I have to at least call Coach Broomes to report my absence, else he might bench me for the next game.

Coach Broomes doesn't believe a vague "sickness" is any excuse to miss practice, not when we're so close to the semifinal on Sunday, so I swallow my pride and tell him that I have period pains.

The silence is loud. And long.

"Coach?" I press the phone closer to my ear. "Are you there? I said I have peri—"

"Girl problems, understood!" And he hangs up.

I don't get it. I've seen Coach Broomes mop up a bloody face with his shirt and pluck knocked-out teeth out of grass, but he gets flustered at the word "period."

Ten minutes later, Daddy bursts into my room with a large basket.

"Don't worry, I was preparing for this," he says, when I sit up. He puts the basket on the bed and pulls out a pack of sanitary napkins.

"These ones 'ere is regular, but we 'ave overnight, ultra thin, these ones 'ere got wings. They suppose to give more protection."

My mouth drops open as Daddy continues to pull what must be the entire shelf of sanitary napkins from the supermarket. He must have overheard my conversation with Coach Broomes.

"Now, yuh know 'ow to put them on?" He arches a bushy eyebrow, but I'm still trying to process the image of my dad surrounded by pads.

"No?" He misinterprets my silence. "Lemme show you; I watch a video." He starts to open the package.

"Daddy, no!" I yell. "I haven't gotten my period yet!"

This is the most embarrassing thing that has ever happened to me.

"So why—"

Understanding dawns on his face, and he sighs and rubs his temples. He does that when he's stressed. And he missed a whole day of work staying home with me. The realization makes me sick with guilt.

"I'm sorry, Daddy. I didn't want to hear anyone talking about the exam results. It's just, I really really want to go to Lamming with Ahkai."

Daddy sits next to me and pulls me against his chest. "I ever tell you about when I first move to Bim?"

I shake my head. Daddy is from Guyana, but he grew up in a fishing village just like Fairy Vale.

"I didn't know not a soul in Barbados, not a soul. But your mother was 'ere, and it make sense fuh me to move. I can fish from anywhere, but she 'ad a nice job in a 'otel restaurant. Me remember the first day being on the dock, feeling lost lost lost. I didn't 'ave no boat, no connections, I didn't know nobody. All I 'ad was my determination to provide for my family. I 'ad to put myself out there, and it work out."

He kisses the top of my head and then fiddles with a braid. It's soon time for him to redo them.

"It's not the same. You're you, and I'm . . . me."

"Bean, you smart and funny, you know that, right?"

"Thanks?" I wait for him to tell me something I don't know.

"You can make new friends easy easy easy. Look 'ow you get on with the cricket team."

Those cricketers like Josephine the bowler, not the person. If I broke my hand, all of them would discard me right away. Everyone except for Jared. But Daddy's shown me how to turn this argument in my favor.

"Queen Mary doesn't have a cricket team!" I declare. I don't know if it's true, but I can't imagine those snobby kids wanting to get sweaty. "Please, Dad, don't make me go."

"I dunno, Lamming so far," he says, pulling away. But I sense the crack in his armor, giving me back my bit of hope.

"No place is far in Barbados, remember?" I shove his words right back in his face. He's always poking fun at how small the island is compared to Guyana.

Daddy scoffs. "You think you smart. But the school bus to Queen Mary does pass right in front of the house. Lamming doesn't 'ave one."

"I could catch the same ride as Ahkai to Lamming," I point out. "And if we have to catch the regular bus, Ahkai and I could walk across town together."

Daddy shoots me a worried look, as if children walking through Bridgetown without parental supervision should be against the law. "The two y'all alone? That's a lot of responsibility."

"Please, Daddy, please."

He sighs. "All right, I'll think about it."

Suddenly, the world is beautiful. The sun is bright in the sky, and the blackbirds' music liven the air. I have the grades for Lamming, so it should be an easy approval.

Little does Daddy know, I plan to pester him every day to make sure he submits that form.

Daddy kisses my forehead again and then gets to his feet. "Come and eat, before you get dark eye in 'ere." That's what he calls getting dizzy.

I step out the bedroom and then pause when a familiar scent invades my nostrils.

"You made cook-up!" I exclaim.

Daddy looks over his shoulder with a cheeky smile.

It's one of my favorite Guyanese dishes—rice and peas with at least three different kinds of meats. You throw everything in the pot with herbs and spices and let it "cook up." Daddy doesn't prepare it very often, but every New Year's Eve, or as he calls it, "Ole Year's Night," he makes a big pot of rice with five different meats, including tripe, chicken feet, and pig tail. It's Guyanese tradition to eat the dish for good luck before the start of the New Year.

I need every bit of luck now to transfer to Lamming . . .

Miss Alleyne, still in teacher mode, knocks on the door and pokes her head into the living room. "Special delivery." She holds a flat silicone bottle in the air.

"It's a hot-water bottle," she says, on seeing our confused expressions. "For the cramps."

I groan and hide my face.

"Don't worry, Rori," Daddy says, bringing the pot of rice to the table. "False alarm."

Now it's Miss Alleyne's turn to be confused, but she catches on quickly. "Ah, okay." She doesn't ask any more questions and takes a seat at the table while Daddy serves the food.

That's her sensei sixth sense power at work again. She can quickly assess and understand any situation. In fact, I asked Daddy if we should tell Miss Alleyne the truth about Mariss, but he said, "It's best to leave the past in the past." Daddy hates conflict, and there's nothing more disagreeable than telling your current girlfriend that your ex was a vicious Sea Mumma who sent lionfish henchmen to kill her in a jealous fit of rage.

I shake the thoughts from my mind.

She is gone. Life goes on.

"This is close to pelau, but with coconut milk and no browning," Miss Alleyne remarks, and then shoves another forkful of rice in her mouth.

"That is what does make all the difference," Daddy replies, and then winks at me. "That, and a secret ingredient."

To her credit, Miss Alleyne doesn't ask what the secret ingredient is.

"Ah, my favorite part!" I heap some blackened rice onto my spoon. It's the burnt grains from the bottom of the pot called "bun-bun."

"This Sunday, I'm gonna make pelau and we gine see whose taste better," she says.

Daddy scoffs. "I gine win."

The whole exchange makes me smile. I don't have many memories of Mum, but she was really competitive, and this is something she might do—a cook-off between the two Caribbean rice dishes.

"Interesting," Miss Alleyne says, checking her phone. "You know how Danielle has that Caribbean cruise this Sunday? Two people just dropped out, and she's asking if we want to go. All expenses paid."

"Whaaat?" Dad and I exclaim.

"I know, right? It's for a week, and goes to Dominica, Saint Vincent, Tobago, Puerto Rico . . ."

My eyes widen at every new country. I've never left Barbados before; we've never been able to afford it.

"Just in time for the start of vacation," Miss Alleyne says, and then she looks up at Dad expectantly. "Vince?"

Daddy gets awkward, clearing his throat. "You and Deirdre could 'ave a good time," he says.

Miss Alleyne sighs and settles back into her seat.

Daddy doesn't want to leave me behind. I'd be alone—Wait a minute! This is the perfect chance to show him I can take care of myself. He'll see that I can be responsible enough for the long journey to Lamming. He won't have any more reasons for me not to attend the school. I knew this cook-up would bring some luck!

"Or *you* could go with her, Dad," I suggest, as if it's a brilliant idea that no one ever thought of.

Dad jerks like he's been hit with a brick. Again, I can't blame him. In a year I've gone from dumping fish guts on his date's head to encouraging him on a romantic Caribbean cruise getaway.

"Who is you, and what you do with my daughter?" he asks.

I lift my chin. "Father, I don't know if you've realized,

but I'm all grown up now. I'll be fine, plus I can sleep by Miss Mo. She won't mind."

But Daddy's still reluctant. "I dunno, the cricket semi-finals ain' this weekend? I can't miss that."

"Daddy, I'll be *fiiiine*. Go and have fun for once. Don't worry about me."

"And we'll be back in time for the finals," Miss Alleyne adds. "And with Jo on the team, we *know* Fairy Vale will make it this year."

Daddy scratches his chin, staring at the wall behind us, while me and Miss Alleyne hold our breaths. Then, he takes up his fork and digs into his cook-up again. "It look like I going on a cruise."

Miss Alleyne cheers, and I join in on the celebration but do my evil laugh in my head.

I plan to stay out of trouble, keep the house spick-and-span, and be the ultimate responsible young lady. When Daddy returns from the cruise, he'll have no more excuses and submit that school transfer to Lamming in no time.

In my mind, I shove Lynne out of the seat next to Ahkai in the classroom at Lamming and take my right-ful place at his side.

CHAPTER 6

For the rest of the week, I carry out Operation Responsible Young Lady, waking up early to make Daddy's favorites for breakfast and cleaning the house, even his dusty old plant pots.

I'm tired and wish I could avoid the church picnic on the north coast today, but Miss Mo has turned it into a celebration event for Ahkai.

I haven't seen much of Ahkai all week; he's been busy with endless interviews, which are basically him staring at the interviewers with a sheepish smile, while Miss Mo answers all the questions. We'd normally carpool to these events, but Miss Mo had to take him to a photo op at the Ministry, so it's just me, Daddy, and Miss Alleyne in Jalopy.

Ahkai's not even at Lamming yet, and the separation has already begun.

I have to fix this before it's too late.

The scenery changes from highways and multiplex buildings to cracked, pothole-filled roads and miles of freshly plowed fields getting prepared for new crops. As we get closer to the park, we pass small corner shops with long lines of people waiting for their Saturday-morning pudding and souse.

It's a nice, peaceful drive, and Miss Alleyne, dressed in one of her African-print dashikis and large sunglasses, starts to snore in the back seat. Daddy and I exchange grins; we're so going to tease her about that later.

Miss Mo's church committee has been wary of beach excursions since Miss Alleyne "nearly drowned," but it's hard to avoid the sea when you live on a small Caribbean island. The park up north is the perfect compromise, with the sea in close view but inaccessible to swimmers. There is a rocky stream where people scavenge for sea whelks—small sea snails. Daddy likes to suck them straight from the shell, but I've never had the courage to try.

We leave Jalopy on a rocky area near the cliffs. The park doesn't look like much—it would never be a stop on an island tour. But at a certain time of year, you can spy humpback whales jumping from the sea, and if you're lucky, sting rays gliding along its surface.

Coach Broomes approaches with his clipboard and a grim face, and in khaki shorts so tight you could count the change in his pockets.

He opens his mouth, maybe to reprimand me for missing practice, but then glances at Miss Alleyne and chooses his words carefully. "Miss Cadogan, I trust everything is in order for you to play tomorrow?"

Heat crawls up my face. I can't meet his eyes, so I just nod and hope that the cliff collapses and takes me with it.

"Ahkai's over there, Jo," says Miss Alleyne, providing the opening for escape.

Thank you, ma'am.

Poor Ahkai is at a picnic table with Lynne, constantly getting approached by the random congregation members we nod at in church. These people hardly used to pay Ahkai attention, and now suddenly he is everyone's favorite cousin/nephew/adopted son. Though there's a half smile on his face, I can tell he desperately wants to be alone by the way his eyes keep darting toward the path where you'd climb down to the river.

Lynne isn't trying to hide her annoyance; she scowls

so hard at a lady who pinches her cheeks that the woman yanks away her hand like it touched a hot oven.

I frown and sit on the opposite side of Ahkai, hoping that between the two of us, we can act as his bodyguards.

It doesn't work.

"And here are the young geniuses! You are truly blessed and highly favored." Pastor Williams, dressed for a Sunday church service rather than a casual picnic, shoves his phone in Lynne's and Ahkai's faces and takes several selfies. He glances at me, as if trying to decide if I'm worth the picture.

"Not her. She didn't pass to Lamming." Lynne smirks and eats a fish cake from the tower of pastries on her plate.

I hope she chokes on a bone.

Pastor Williams looks at me with pity and squeezes my shoulder. "Oh dear, I'm sure you did your best."

"I passed to Queen Mary. It's a top school too!" I say, louder than I had intended.

Behind Pastor Williams, Daddy beams at me and gives me a thumbs-up. *Oh no . . .* hopefully he doesn't think I changed my mind about the transfer.

I seethe all through the picnic, growing more and more annoyed with every enthusiastic "congratulations" to Lynne and Ahkai. Not even the food: rice and black-eyed peas, macaroni pie, shepherd's pie, roast pork, chicken patties, jam puffs—none of it—improves my mood.

Finally, we get a chance to head down by the river—and I'm miffed that Lynne is now included in my "we." Ahkai sits on the riverbed and pulls out his whittling tools. Lynne plunges her hands into the pebbly sand and starts to collect shells. I spy a large rock with a natural bull's-eye—perfect for bowling practice. For a while, we occupy ourselves in comfortable silence; I hate that Lynne fits so well into our peace.

Then Lynne snaps her head toward the edge of the river, by a few fat pork trees. My body grows tense as I follow her gaze—something is moving under the pebbles.

"*Chelonioidea*," Lynne whispers. Her voice has lost its flat tone and is full of wonder.

"What?" I ask, stepping closer to Ahkai.

Ahkai stops whittling and gapes at Lynne, repeating the same word.

"Colonia-what?!"

A tiny baby turtle crawls out of the sand. It walks in a circle on shaky flippers. Five more baby turtles crawl out of the hole and head to the water.

"Chelonioidea. Sea turtle, in Latin," Ahkai clarifies for me.

Oh great, she's a Latin language lover too.

Lynne is surprised Ahkai knows the language, and then, her cross face becomes almost pleasant as they gaze at each other with admiration. My last thread of patience snaps. Their best-friendship is developing before my very eyes.

I open my mouth to shout, scream, chastise Ahkai and Lynne for—for what? Living in the same house? Understanding Latin? Getting into Lamming school? They didn't do any of those things to spite me. The anger fades away, leaving me feeling very tired and . . . broken. I sigh, and my chest folds like it's been punctured with a screwdriver.

Ahkai glances at me and cocks his head.

I can't talk to him about my feelings, especially with Lynne right here, though she's busy helping one of the baby turtles to the water. Trust she'd show a gentle side at this moment when I'm feeling so rotten.

Without saying a word, I turn and march along the riverbank, needing to be alone. This time, Ahkai doesn't follow.

As I move farther away from the coast, the stream gets smaller and the rocks jagged, but more crab shells crunch under my feet. The hermit crabs leave them behind when they outgrow them.

Just like how Ahkai will abandon me.

The thought punches me in the gut so hard I double over. After that, I try to keep my mind blank, walking and bowling pebbles at trees, until I notice the fading sunlight. It's time to return to the picnic.

I glance around, trying to find my bearings. *Where did the river go?* I listen for the sound of water trickling on rocks, but there's nothing but wind blowing through trees. I'm on a pasture with large patches of dirt and a few tufts of bush in the distance. *Maybe there are fat pork trees?* The fruit trees grow close to the park, so I head toward them.

I stop in my tracks when I turn by the bushy trees. There's a dirt road ahead with tire tracks in the middle, but thick fields of sugarcane swallow the path.

The danger of my situation hits me at once: I am in the north of the island, lost and alone near a cane field, with darkness about to fall.

The Heartman.

He would rub his decaying hands with delight. No need for him to start up his hearse—a fresh, young heart has been delivered right to his door. My mind returns to the moment at the breadfruit roast, not the one where Miss Mo rambles about insect-ridden coats and stinky breath, but Aunt Jackie's sad face and her solemn *I remember those days.* Now I've put myself into a position where she could one day tell people about me at another community roast. *I remember that girl Josephine.*

After everything I went through last year, I would be foolish to dismiss the Heartman stories. I back away from the cane fields slowly.

A clinking noise rises in the air. Some kind of chain, brushing against hollow wood? No, not wood, a stalk of cane.

Then, heavy footsteps stomp toward me. I whirl around and sprint across the pasture, my fear blocking out everything but my panicked breaths.

The grass grows thinner, changing into an uneven, rocky surface. My feet slip and slide in my slippers. Of all days not to wear sneakers! I glance back as I run, expecting to see a tall man in a flapping black cloak behind me. I finally stop and catch my breath behind a large rock, my hand pressed against my chest, willing my heart to slow down. I'm sure the Heartman can hear the beats and use it to find me, like GPS.

I take another peek; still no sign of anyone. But it's not dark yet, maybe he has to wait until all the light disappears to strike. I have no idea where I am, but there's the edge of a cliff and the sea in the distance. If I follow the ocean, there's a good chance it will lead me to a road, but I doubt I can find help before nightfall.

Then, I hear the most beautiful sound. A car engine! And the crunch of tires on rocks. I leap to my feet, already waving to get attention.

A long black vehicle comes into view, driving slowly along the rocks.

A hearse! My hand drops to my side, and I get ready to bolt again. But where can I go? My options are toward the hearse or off the cliffs. I can choose to get my heart ripped from my chest, or my body splattered onto the rocks. Either way, my death would be very, very bloody. Are these really my options now? Be a fillet or a pancake?

As I debate the terrible choice, I glance back at the vehicle. A sleek bumper with silver grilles comes into view, shiny enough to create its own light in the fading sun.

Not a hearse.

"Oh, thank goodness." I wave at the car and hurry toward it, in case the driver decides to leave me stranded. Daddy always warns me not to get into a car with strangers, but this is one time I'll make an exception.

Someone opens the car door and steps outside.

"Mr. Atkins!" I exclaim. I've never been so happy to see him, even though he's frowning down at me. He's wearing one of his brown shirt-jacs, but this time with old, faded jeans and dirty boots. The drab outfit clashes with his flashy car.

"I got lost! Can you take me back to the church picnic?"

Mr. Atkins remains silent, staring at me until I become uncomfortable, shifting my feet on the rocks. "Mr. Atkins?"

He shakes his head. "Get in."

I pause for a second, and then dash to the car, eager to get back to Daddy and farther away from the cane fields.

Mr. Atkins doesn't attempt to make small talk, and neither do I. Inside the car is as fancy as the outside. It is brand-new, like it was made yesterday, with black leather seats and a high-tech dashboard that is more fitting for a plane than a car.

But the artificial cherry air freshener can't mask an odd, earthy scent, like a cow pasture after a storm.

I check the mats, but there's not a speck of dirt on them. Nor on my slippers.

The smell grows stronger by the second, and I hold my breath and don't release it until we get back to the park.

CHAPTER 7

I had hoped Mr. Atkins would just drop me off at the park and leave, but he marches up to Daddy to inform him that he stumbled upon his daughter lost and scared up North Point.

Mr. Atkins glances across at Miss Alleyne at the picnic table and then sneers at Daddy. "Maybe if you weren't so preoccupied you would have realized she was missing."

To say Daddy isn't pleased is an understatement. He is silent as he looks me over to make sure I'm unhurt, but his disapproval hums in the air. All of my "responsible young lady" efforts this week go right down the drain.

I avoid Daddy's eyes and spot Ahkai coming up from the river, his face bent with worry. He slips on one of the rocks, but luckily, Lynne is there to steady him. Ahkai spots me by the table and exhales with relief and makes his way to me. Lynne seems disappointed that I am alive, but she shrugs and heads to the food table.

"And I'm still waiting on those final reports, Miss Alleyne. Make sure they're in my inbox before you go on your love boat."

"I hear you, Mr. Atkins," Miss Alleyne replies, in a cold, flat voice.

Miss Mo appears next to Mr. Atkins and grabs his arm. "Mr. Atkins, just the man I want to see. The committee needs a favor." She hustles him to the table of church women with large hats.

Daddy waits 'til he's out of earshot to unleash. "Josephine Cadogan, you tell me you gine down by the river! 'Ow you end up at North Point?"

"Daddy, I only went for a walk. I wasn't gone more than half hour!" I lie. Ahkai nods, backing me up, without any prompting at all. This is why he's my best friend.

"That is foolishness, Josephine! You don't know up 'ere. You cudda get snatch up!"

He doesn't know the half of it. There's no way I'll say a word about the rattling chain in the cane field; I'm already "foolish," no need to add "paranoid" or "traumatized" to the list.

"I got two mind about this cruise now," Daddy says, his nostrils flaring.

He can't mean that. There's no way he'd disappoint Miss Alleyne, not the day before the cruise. But his words still make me nervous.

"I'll be fine, please, I promise!" I send Ahkai a look of desperation; he knows Operation Responsible Young Lady is in jeopardy.

"I will keep her safe, Uncle Vince," Ahkai says, to everyone's surprise.

The "Uncle Vince" is a masterful touch that melts some of Daddy's annoyance away. A smile slides onto his face, and he squeezes Ahkai's shoulder. "I know you will, son."

Just when I'm about to relax, Miss Alleyne speaks up. "Actually, I was thinking we shouldn't go anymore. It doesn't feel right to leave now."

"Ma'am, you *have* to go!" I cry, panicking. If she and Daddy stay home, there is no way he will sign the form in time, not when I haven't proven I'm responsible.

"Yuh sure, Rori?" Daddy's face is creased with concern. "You been at work hard, you could use a lil vacation."

She sighs and rubs her forehead, and removes her

sunglasses, revealing dark circles under her eyes. "I'm fine. I've just been trying to finish these reports that the head of the department *suddenly* requested."

She glares at Mr. Atkins, who is now at the food table, chastising Lynne about the amount of desserts on her plate. He removes some of her jam puffs and currant slices. Then he mutters something to Coach Broomes, waiting in the line behind him, and glowers at Miss Alleyne.

"Okay, ma'am, what's going on between you and Mr. Atkins?"

She sighs. "Remember all those stories about my cadet sergeant? The one I ambushed in the gully? He's the one who told me the army was no place for a woman."

I nod, and she arches an eyebrow.

"That was Mr. Atkins?!" I yelp.

Miss Alleyne shushes me.

I can't believe my previous form teacher is the person who crushed Miss Alleyne's dreams all those years ago. And now he's back, trying to make her life miserable again.

"Me don't like 'ow that man treat you," Daddy says, frowning at Mr. Atkins and then tucking his arm into hers. "Don't let 'im steal your joy, you know."

I nod. "You don't want to miss hiking to the Pitons in Saint Lucia, right? Or the underwater sculpture park in Grenada. The black sand beaches in Martinique."

She's been talking about these activities all week. She deserves to go on this trip, and Daddy too. I'm not just thinking about myself and my attempt to transfer to Lamming either. Daddy's worked hard all his life and never spends a dime on himself. Besides, who knows when he'd be able to afford an opportunity like this?

"You're so right," Miss Alleyne replies, and then gives Daddy a tired smile. "We better leave now so I can pack and finish these reports . . . maybe even get some sleep."

I exhale with relief.

Danger averted. Operation Responsible Young Lady is still a go.

We say our goodbyes, and I make an effort to be on my best behavior, thanking everyone for the delicious food, especially the sweet, smiling gran who gives kids those strawberry hard candies at church.

Daddy takes another way home, this time driving past endless fields of sugarcane. The stalks seem to whisper threats as Jalopy zooms by, and I close my eyes until the smell of the air changes from sweet soil to the car exhaust fumes of the city and finally, the salty sea scent of Fairy Vale.

I try to forget all about the rattling chain and footsteps, but that night, I lay in bed staring at the ceiling, unable to sleep because I keep reliving the moment in front of the cane fields.

It could have been a cow or goat chained to a fence somewhere nearby. Those footsteps could have come from anyone—a farmer checking on his crops, a teenager stealing a stalk of cane, even another lost kid.

Of course that immediately makes me think about a child's body parts in a bag.

I shiver and wrap myself tighter in my blanket, but then a blue circle flashes by my bedroom window. I rub my eyes, and then several blue dots appear, glowing and blinking like a clock that needs resetting.

That's odd.

I get up and pull aside the curtain.

The road is empty—nothing but the shadows of trees swaying in the wind. But the hairs on the back of my neck stand on end. Miss Alleyne is always advising me to trust my instincts, though I may need a few more years for mine to become as good as hers. A red alert goes off inside my brain. Something is terribly wrong;

the night feels heavy, as if something is holding the darkness hostage.

I grab my trusty binoculars from the dresser and survey the area, but nothing stands out.

Even the sky is empty; it is a dreary, starless night.

The brass clock strikes three, its echo saying, "here we go again." The last time I had insomnia, Mariss was lurking outside my door, planning to kill me in my sleep.

She is gone. Life goes on.

I slide back into bed and repeat the mantra in my head. Soon, my eyelids grow heavier and heavier, and I drift off to sleep.

Sometime later—it could be minutes or hours—the rain starts to fall, blowing my curtains into the air and sending cold raindrops across my face. It's odd . . . the rain rarely comes through my bedroom window.

I will myself to get out from under the sheets, cracking my eyes open just enough to make my way to the window, trying not to lose the sleep. As soon as I reach the window, the rain stops. I groan under my breath and then, even though my eyes are almost shut, I notice an odd shadow by the bus stop in front of Miss Mo's house.

I'm still groggy, but for some reason the dark spot holds my attention. The shadow moves closer to the dim streetlight, revealing the shape of some kind of horse? It would be the largest horse I've ever seen in my life, maybe it's a bull? Whatever it is, it's way bigger than Jalopy. A chain around its neck glints, and it's only when a hand tugs on the chain that I realize that the bus stop above the shadow isn't a bus stop at all.

It is a man . . . sitting on the animal's back? The man is very tall, taller than any person I know, and so still he could be a statue.

Wake up, now! My brain screams, and I try to fully open my eyes . . . but I can't.

My heart should be racing with fright, but the beats slow down, like someone else is pulling the strings. I press my hand against my chest, trying to protect my heart, trying to regain some control.

What if I jumped out the window? The thought comes out of nowhere in a voice that sounds like me but is definitely *not* mine. That's a terrible idea; I'd break a few bones for sure. But it's so cool outside, and I really really need a breath of fresh air.

I stick my head out the window, tilt my chin to the sky, and the wind whips through my braids. That's much better, but the rest of my body is so hot. All I need to do is climb—

A cat's meow breaks the silence of the night.

What am I doing? I grab hold of the ledge to stop myself from falling through. I slide down to the floor in my bedroom, my bare knees scraping against the wood.

The last thing I remember, before everything goes black, is my hand reaching to close the window.

CHAPTER 8

The sunlight burns my cheek. I turn my face into the pillow and end up with a mouthful of dust bunnies.

I splutter and sit up, slapping away the clumps of dust from my face. This is what I get for being too lazy to take the dustpan downstairs and emptying it behind my bedroom curtains instead.

But why am I out of bed? Did I sleepwalk across the room? I sit under the windowsill, confused for a few seconds, until a blurred memory of a shadowed man returns to me. I gasp and snap my head up—the window is closed.

I grip the windowsill and slowly peer out at the bus stop.

There's nothing there.

Still, I can't bring myself to open the window to let in fresh air. Did I really try to climb through the window last night, or was that part of the strange dream?

My mind races with blurred images, so fast I can't grab hold of any of them. With the Heartman stories from the breadfruit roast, and the incident in the cane fields, it's no surprise I'm dreaming about creepy figures. I frown and try my best to remember any specific details about the man, but nothing comes to mind.

And I am so, so tired. I went to bed around three—I remember the clock! Now it's after 6:00 a.m., so that's only three hours of rest. That explains my fatigue but not the chest pains. I rub my chest and wince. It feels like someone bowled a cricket ball at my heart.

Cricket! Today is the semifinal of the competition. I can't afford to be in less than perfect form! And Daddy's leaving today too . . .

I return to bed, determined to get in a few more hours so I can put in a good performance for the team. I can't let paranoia and bad dreams stop me from making it to the finals.

Daddy wakes me up a few hours later for Sunday breakfast with a giant smile on his face. His favorite reggae tunes fill the air, and he shimmies to the door doing that cheesy, broken-foot dance that makes me want to disown him. "Pancakes ready!"

I take one last glance outside the window and then follow him downstairs.

As we eat, he chatters on about the cruise and the places he hopes we can travel to together. I try to listen, but I'm too troubled by thoughts of shadowy creatures and thick chains.

"Bean?" Daddy asks, gently touching my hand.

He must have asked me a question.

"Sorry, Daddy, what?"

He cocks his head. "Something wrong?"

My confession about the dream is on the tip of my tongue, but I swallow it. He's so excited about this trip— if I mention anything about nightmares or sleepwalking, there's no way he'll get on that boat. And there's also Operation Responsible Young Lady. He still has to sign the transfer to Lamming school. I can't risk all this because I *think* I saw something weird outside the house.

"Just thinking about my game strategy," I say, and put a giant chunk of pancake in my mouth.

"I sorry I 'ave to miss it," Daddy says, slumping down into his chair. "But I know y'all gine win. The finals won't miss me. I gine come right to the stadium as soon as the cruise ship dock. The group was planning to do some salsa dancing—" Then he sighs. "Watch me going on and on about the cruise. Is just that—me ain' travel since . . ." His voice trails away.

"Your honeymoon?" I finish the sentence, and Daddy nods. A wave of sadness comes over his face.

I grab his hand and give it a quick squeeze. "Mum would be happy that you're happy."

Daddy's entire face brightens, and he pokes me in that ticklish spot in my ribs. After that, I don't let anything distract me from our last few moments together.

An hour later, I'm outside in my Fairy Vale cricket uniform, a white-and-blue shirt and long white pants. Daddy lifts suitcases into the taxi since the driver, Bernard, a hairy-faced man who's always chewing on a matchstick—and hopefully not the same one—charges extra for handling luggage.

It's a thirty-minute ride to the port without traffic, but Bernard is known for stopping at a rum shop in the middle of the journey for a quick game of dominoes, so Daddy and Miss Alleyne are leaving early.

Daddy slams the trunk closed. "That is everything," he says, and then smiles at me. "Unless my Bean want to sneak in my bag."

Suddenly, my eyes and nose start to burn. I take a deep

breath to hold it together. Saying goodbye is harder than I thought. I've never spent a day without Daddy; this time he'll be gone for an entire seven days. Despite my efforts, a tear escapes my eye, and I wipe it away before anyone sees.

Miss Alleyne puts a hand on my shoulder. "We'll check in every day."

I nod, still not trusting myself to speak.

Bernard honks his horn in impatience, though he is literally an arm's length away.

Daddy bends down to hug me. I bury my head in his chest, and we don't let go.

Bernard sucks his teeth. "You only gine 'way for couple days, right? 'Cause wunna acting like he going off to war."

Daddy breaks the hug to scowl at him. Miss Alleyne gives me one last shoulder squeeze and then gets into the back of the taxi.

Daddy goes to join her but then turns to me again.

"You finish—"

"Bag's already packed."

Daddy pats his pants pocket. "And the cruise—"

"Schedule and information is taped on the fridge." *As if I don't have it memorized by now.*

"All right, I—"

"Love you too."

Daddy smiles and gets in the car. "My big girl got everything under control."

My grin drops a bit. I know I'm trying to prove I'm responsible, but I just want to be his little girl in this moment.

Bernard beeps the horn again and speeds off before Daddy can close the door properly. I stay on the curb and watch the taxi disappear before going back inside.

The silence isn't a peaceful one; it is eerie. Daddy only left with one suitcase, but he might as well have taken all the furniture because the house is empty without him.

As a reflex, I glance at the TV stand, where a picture of Mum—the *only* picture of her—used to be before Mariss took the frame to "the cleaners" and never returned it.

I touch Mum's flower-print handkerchief in my pocket instead, and the piece of silk brings some comfort. I take a deep breath and survey the living room, relishing in my newfound independence . . . which lasted all of two seconds before Miss Mo bursts open the door.

"Jo, why you taking so long to get 'cross the road?" she demands, her hands on her hips. "I gine drop you off at the game and then head to the fish market."

"Coming, Miss Mo," I reply, and swing my backpack

with my toiletries and clothing over my shoulder.

As we cross the road and Miss Mo complains about the price of uniforms, my eyes zero in on the bus stop. It's about seven feet tall but looks short compared to the blurry shadow. There are no footprints in the mud, no leaves on the ground, nothing.

"Miss Mo?" I interrupt her. "What does the Heartman actually look like? Is he a giant? Like, way taller than this bus stop?"

As always, Miss Mo's face lights up at the chance to talk about scary folklore. "Jo, I can't help yuh, nobody who see what he look like live to tell the tale. You understand how evil he is?"

"But how would someone fight him?" I ask quickly, before she goes into a descriptive monologue about the Heartman's evilness.

"Don't be outside after dark."

"But what if you happen to stumble onto him, Miss Mo? What could you do then?"

"Run. Run as fast as you can." Miss Mo's eyes dart around, as if she's checking to make sure the Heartman doesn't jump out from behind her hedges. Then she beckons for me to follow her inside.

In the kitchen, Miss Mo rifles through a basket of spices. She opens a box of Oxo seasoning and starts to remove the foil-covered cubes. Then, when she gets near the bottom of the box, she pulls out a translucent crystal tied to a piece of brown cooking string.

She presses it into my hand. "This gine protect you from evil," she says, in a hushed voice. "Put it on."

I wait until Miss Mo ducks her head into the larder to shove the crystal in the side pouch of my backpack; there's no way I'm removing my necklace with Ahkai's hummingbird pendant.

"And don't forget old faithful." Miss Mo reappears clutching a bag of black-eyed peas. I groan and glance at the entrance, praying that Lynne doesn't choose this moment to step into the kitchen. I'm sure black-eyed peas can't protect anyone, especially from a cursed man with a knack for ripping out hearts, but I still put some peas into my pockets and backpack.

"We better leave now, before it gets too late," I say, checking my watch. "I'll get Ahkai."

"Ahkai?" Miss Mo replies. "He left here ever since. He gone to the beach with Lynne."

CHAPTER 9

I usually enjoy the journey to my cricket matches. My body tingles with anticipation, eager to get onto the field and cause havoc. Daddy and Miss Alleyne encourage my excitement, all of us teasing one another, and the drive is full of fun and laughs. But today, even with Miss Mo chattering in the background, I am overcome by the weight of loneliness.

One day you could be making plans about your future school with your bestie, and the next day, he could be off saving sea turtles with a new best friend. And now that Daddy and Miss Alleyne are on the cruise, no one will be cheering for me in the stands today.

Miss Mo drops me off by the ice cream truck parked outside the school. Up ahead, Casper is at his spot by the school gate using the giant foam finger to sweep a squashed can. He's in his Sunday best, which is his normal khaki shirt and shorts but with a black bow tie. The can lands on the gravel with a soft clatter, and Casper drags it to the trash.

I stop dead in my tracks; the sound of the rattling can jogs a memory. Dread washes over my body, and my throat goes painfully dry.

On the night Casper had his breakdown, he claimed the Heartman was *riding a steel donkey*. It's a cursed animal with eyes like fire. Legend says a steel donkey is after you when you hear chains dragging in the night.

Miss Mo said no one who saw the Heartman survived to tell the tale, but someone possibly did. *Casper.* The incident may have damaged his mind, but he's still alive.

Casper is trying, and failing, to get the can into the bin with the foam finger. I pluck it from the ground and toss it into the trash.

"Casper." My voice cracks, so I swallow and try again. "Casper, can I ask you something? Please."

"Ah, the young warrior!" Then he whispers into his favorite twig. "One of the more intelligent members of the pride."

"Casper, can you tell me what happened . . . the night your wife disappeared?"

Casper blinks twice. "It is time for my sustenance. I shall feast on white grains, the wings of a roasted fowl, and a cup of squashed lemons." He drops the foam finger into the trash and ambles away.

"Casper! Casper!" I trail after him, but he ignores me. "Did you see the Heartman? And the steel donkey? Hear rattling chains?"

He hums the *Dora the Explorer* theme song and wraps his four long, gray locs around his head. Like everyone else, he wants to forget and move on, but if I've learned anything from my ordeal last year, it's that trauma doesn't go away when you pretend it doesn't exist.

Years ago, Casper had a popular radio show. The whole island tuned in to hear his social commentary, interviews, and music playlists. Daddy told me his name once. What was it? It rhymed with a body organ. Face? Belly? Kidney?

"Sidney!" I shout.

Casper stops walking, but he doesn't turn around. Does he even recognize his real name? I bet no one has called him Sidney in years.

"Sidney," I repeat, hurrying in front of him. "Please, talk to me. Tell me what happened that day. Your wife. What was her name?"

Casper stares blankly ahead, as if I'm invisible. A few

seconds pass without him even blinking. Like someone flicked his "off" switch. Who am I kidding? This man and his thoughts are broken. I drop my shoulders and turn away.

"Jennifer."

The voice is so soft I almost don't recognize it's Casper who spoke the name.

"Jennifer," he repeats, this time with a sad smile. Gone is his loud, projected radio accent. His wife's name feels like a soft touch on my cheek.

"She was an artist. One of the best topiarists in the Caribbean," he continues. He twirls his twig between his fingers.

I can't believe it; Casper is speaking understandable English.

"She used to create masterpieces from the hedges of our lawn, any animal at all, only with some bush and a scissors."

An ache grows in my chest as he strokes his twig. I am so so so ashamed for laughing at him in the past.

"The Heartman came at midnight, burst into our yard, astride the steel donkey. Jennifer tried to fight him, but her shears went right through his black cloak, as if he were made out of thick smoke. I tried to save her, I tried, but it happened so fast. I—"

He closes his eyes in pain, and his jaw twitches as the rest of the words fight to get out. Who knows how long they've been kept inside, but I don't push him to finish. Like me, those words have to wait until he's good and ready to share them.

Casper peers at something over my shoulder. "Do my eyes deceive me, or is that a four-legged scavenger in the distance?"

It's actually a garbage truck.

Casper has returned.

He squints through the twig. "Fascinating, so rare to see it traversing this territory during daylight. I must investigate."

I watch him sprint toward the garbage truck, my insides still swirling with emotions. Mostly fear. The shadowed creature outside my window was not a dream.

This can't be happening to me, not again. This is Fairy Vale. A village where people wear their best clothes to the market because there's nowhere else to go. Why don't monsters choose a more interesting place to terrorize? In movies, all the monsters go to California and New York, maybe Japan, why do they keep ending up in a tiny village in Barbados?

My brain, sensing a complete meltdown, scrambles to

find a rational explanation, but I won't waste any more time denying the truth.

I went up north and returned with more than leftovers.

The Heartman must have followed me back to Fairy Vale.

CHAPTER 10

I stare without seeing, still frozen to the spot. Why would the Heartman choose me as his next victim? I don't go outside after dark, and I don't cause much trouble—not anymore.

A loud whistle breaks through my daze.

The game! It's clear what I have do *now*, and that's play cricket. I can worry about everything else later. I take a deep breath, put on my game face, and march through the gates.

The crowd is already cheering with loud drums beating in the stands. Our opponents, Stonehall, are stretching on the field, but the Fairy Vale team is huddled together in the bleachers with worried expressions. Jared paces nearby with a cell phone to his ear.

"What's going on?" I ask, and a few of them answer with shrugs.

To my surprise, Mr. Atkins comes from behind the bleachers, dressed in a white polo shirt and pants and holding a clipboard. His face is so sour there should be a lemon in his mouth instead of a pen.

"Miss Cadogan, you decide to grace us with your presence." He checks his watch. "Two minutes late. You!" Mr. Atkins points at the substitute boy with the flat-top, and he jumps to his feet. "Take her place. Cadogan, you're on the bench today."

My mouth drops open in shock. "We haven't even started to warm up yet!" He can't be serious. *Where is Coach Broomes?*

Jared hurries over. "Mr. Atkins, she's our best bowler, we need her."

"Then she should have been here on time."

Mr. Atkins crosses out something on the team sheet— probably my name—and heads over to the match referee.

"I'm sorry, Jo, Coach won't pick up his phone, and he made himself assistant coach." Jared huffs and glares at Mr. Atkins. You know he's mad 'cause no way Jared would show blatant disrespect for a teacher. I wish Miss

Alleyne were here; she would put Mr. Atkins in his place.

There's nothing to do but watch the game from the sidelines. I growl in frustration whenever a Stonehall player hits a ball for six runs. We're getting slaughtered out there, all because of Mr. Atkins's vendetta against female cricketers. Say what you want about Coach Broomes, but he would never jeopardize winning such an important match because of a fragile ego.

Crack! One of the Stonehall batsmen strikes the ball right back at a Fairy Vale bowler, and it crashes into his head. A low moan echoes in the stands. *That's gotta hurt.*

The game stops while the emergency officials tend to the boy, and minutes later, they declare he will be fine but unable to continue playing. For a second, it seems like Mr. Atkins might choose the second substitute boy, but then he gives me a curt nod. I rush onto the field before he can change his mind.

Jared throws me the ball. "You got this."

I take a deep breath, rub the ball against my pants to get extra bounce, and race down the pitch to bowl.

Crack!

The batsman mistimes the ball and hits it high into

the air. With a burst of speed, I race toward the ball and take a leaping dive forward, catching it in my fingertips.

My face is pressed against the field, tasting soil and grass. The crowd cheers, but I lay still, waiting for the umpire to confirm it's a legal catch. I raise my head to see two Stonehall players glowering above me.

"Cheater!" One of the batsmen points his bat at my butt. I glance down; a couple of black-eyed peas roll from my pocket and join the others that have spilled onto the grass.

"This is clear ball tampering!" the other scowling player shouts. "She rubbed the ball against those peas to make scratches. No wonder she got so much bounce."

My breath hitches in my throat, and I scramble to my feet. If I'm found guilty of ball tampering, that's a suspension, or worse, being kicked off the team. But how can I explain that I have the black-eyed peas to ward off evil spirits?

"They're for good luck!" I yelp.

The crowd gets restless and starts to boo. I hide my face in my shirt while the umpires examine the ball. Why can't evil spirits be afraid of oats, marshmallows, or *any* soft food item that can't leave scratches on the ball?

After some back-and-forth, the umpires decide to

call it a no ball, but I have to be replaced with a substitute player. Mr. Atkins doesn't put up one iota of fight against the decision. I avoid his face, but I can feel him sneering at me on the bench. If we lose, now he'll have someone to blame.

Me.

I'm almost too ashamed to watch the rest of the game from the stands. I will not cry. I won't give him the satisfaction. Now I'm glad Daddy, Miss Alleyne, and Ahkai aren't here to witness my humiliation.

In the end, Fairy Vale wins the match by five runs.

We're headed to the finals.

I exhale and lean back on the bench. But instead of rushing onto the field to celebrate with the rest of the team, I stay in the seat, still fighting back tears of guilt, anger, and relief.

A few minutes later, Jared sits next to me in the bleachers.

"Sorry I wasn't much help today," I say, my face to the ground.

He looks puzzled. "It's a win for the team, which means it's a win for everyone, that includes you."

It's true, but it still doesn't lift my spirits. I scoff, "I never thought I would miss Coach Broomes."

Jared's face drops, and I regret the words immediately.

He and Coach are close; he must be worried sick.

"I'm sure Coach is fine," I reassure him, and he nods.

The words don't seem good enough. His other hand is very close to mine. All I have to do is move it an inch to the right to squeeze his for comfort, or give two sympathy pats. I move my finger closer, millimeter by millimeter, until the edge of my finger touches his, ever so slightly. Then I immediately chicken out and move away my hand.

Jared doesn't react; he probably didn't notice. I'm an idiot for feeling disappointed. Then, to my surprise, Jared rests his hand on top of mine. A warm feeling settles in my belly and suddenly I am energized—I could bowl ten straight overs without a break.

"I hope you're coming to Adam's birthday party later," Jared says. "DJ Hypa Tension is going to be there."

Who the heck is Adam? Jared sees my confusion and gestures to the substitute player with the flattop. I try to commit his name to memory.

"I don't think I was invited."

"There you go again. He invited the team. You're part of the team."

Jared has been encouraging me to hang out with the other cricketers outside of matches and practice. I can only turn down so many invitations before he gets offended, but he doesn't understand. I've never been out with a group of kids my own age before; my friend circle is just me and Ahkai. I guess that's more of a line than a circle. Jared is funny, nice, talented, and popular—it's easy for people like him to fit in. He never has to worry about saying the wrong things or embarrassing himself.

I don't reply, and the longer I take to answer, the more awkward it gets. I hate watching the brightness fade from his eyes.

"The boys don't like me, Jared."

"That's not true!" he insists. "They just don't know you."

"I don't see why I need to force myself on people," I reply, getting irritated and turning away.

"Not *people*, your teammates. Besides, *I* like you."

All of my irritation drains away and my stomach goes flippity-flop, as if the organs inside are bowling fastballs. I risk a peek at Jared, and he has a shy smile on his face.

Say something, my brain screams, but I can't get any words out of my mouth. Suddenly, I feel the urge to be anywhere but here.

"I'm sorry," I choke, and sprint toward the girls' dressing room.

There, I replay the moment, upset with myself for

acting so foolish. I wish I could talk to someone about my crush on Jared.

My crush?

I groan and put my head in my lap.

I like *like* him.

How did I not recognize it before? Now what am I going to do? I don't even think I'm allowed to have a crush. How will I break the news to Daddy?

I don't have time for a crush, especially not with a potential monster lurking about the village. I should be on my way home to tell Ahkai about the Heartman and formulate some kind of defense in case he attacks, not hiding in a bathroom to process *feelings*. This is the worst possible time for butterflies in the belly.

Still, I stay in the bathroom until I believe almost everyone has left, but when I finally emerge, I'm surprised to see all of the team still in the bleachers, along with Mr. Atkins, Principal Clarke, and two police officers.

I hurry over to join them.

"Don't freak out," Jared says before I can ask any questions. "But Coach Broomes is missing."

CHAPTER 11

Under Principal Clarke's supervision, Constable Cumberbatch and Constable Jones question us about the last time we saw Coach Broomes.

There's no way I'm going to tell them he was inquiring about my fake period pains. When it's my turn, I just describe what he was wearing at the picnic; lucky for them (and unlucky for me), those khaki pants are burned into memory.

"You may be the last person here to have seen him," says Constable Jones. "He never returned home from the picnic. His wife reported him missing today."

"Coach Broomes is married?!" I blurt out, and then cover my mouth.

There is a flicker of recognition in Constable

Cumberbatch's eyes as he narrows them at me. I lower my head, hoping he won't remember that he caught me roaming the streets after dark last year.

"You think something bad happened to Coach?" Jared asks, his face lined with worry. I wish I was next to him so I could squeeze his hand again.

Constable Jones attempts to reassure him. "We're just making early inquiries; it hasn't even been a full twenty-four hours yet. It's very likely Sean went out with friends and forgot to inform the missus."

We all exchange grave looks. Coach Broomes has never, ever missed a practice session, much less a game.

Wait a minute . . . I wasn't the last person to see Coach Broomes. Mr. Atkins spoke to him at the picnic too. I glance at him, waiting for him to speak up, and happen to catch a movement that sends a shiver down my spine.

Mr. Atkins smiled.

Not wide enough to show any teeth, and so fleeting you could blink and miss it, but he smiled.

Is he happy about Coach Broomes's disappearance since he'd be the new cricket coach? Or is it something more sinister? All these strange occurrences started as soon as he came back into town. And he's different too . . . meaner and more bitter. Then I recall that overwhelming dirty smell in his car. Not strong enough to give me a sore throat, like Miss Mo said about the Heartman's scent, but it's definitely suspicious. My eyes zero in on Mr. Atkins's empty hands.

"Is Coach Broomes's clipboard missing too?" I ask, and everyone goes silent.

Constable Cumberbatch frowns. "Young lady, this is no time for jokes."

"I'm not joking!" I protest. "Coach Broomes never goes anywhere without it. If his clipboard is at home, he's definitely been kidnapped."

To my relief, the other cricketers murmur in agreement.

I glance back at Mr. Atkins, and he gives me one of his death stares. Coach Broomes's clipboard is deep brown and stained, with a clip so rusty it's likely a health hazard. *Where is that clipboard Mr. Atkins had earlier? I need to examine it.*

Constable Cumberbatch glowers at me. "You." He finally remembers me. "You always causing trouble."

I decide to keep my mouth shut; the police won't take me seriously. There's no way I can tell them my suspicions about Mr. Atkins. Nobody listens to almost-twelve-year-olds, even when their lives depend on it.

"I'm sure Coach Broomes will be back with us soon,"

says Principal Clarke. "But until then, I'll leave you in Mr. Atkins's capable hands."

Then she escorts the policemen away, leaving us innocent kids in the "capable hands" of a potential murderer.

"Fall in, troops," he says in his firm tone. "The cricket final is in one hundred sixty-five hours, so we don't have time to waste. And from your performance today, you need all the practice, starting now."

"But but," Jared splutters. "We just finished a match."

"The correct response is 'Yes, sir,'" Mr. Atkins barks, causing us all to jump. "Let's start with a small warm-up, beginning with ten laps around the field."

And then he begins one of the most grueling training sessions we have ever had. After the laps, Mr. Atkins makes us do push-ups, planks, and crawl across the cricket field on our arms and bellies. After his training session, a ninety-year-old granny could beat any of us in a twenty-meter sprint. The team hobbles off the field, groaning at soreness in muscles we didn't know existed. Poor DJ Hypa Tension; no one will be dancing at the party this evening. The boys will probably sit around, massaging their feet with Benjie's Balm to the latest calypso tunes.

The sun is already disappearing from the sky; I need to get indoors.

I slip away without anyone noticing, casting one last regretful look at Jared, who is passing out water to the other cricketers. My legs are way too sore for walking. The Transport Board bus runs on its own schedule on Sundays, but maybe it will actually come on time.

I'm near the school gates when Mr. Atkins calls my name in the distance. There's no one else around, and his tone isn't friendly at all—it's threatening. There's no way I'm facing him alone, not when he could be a supernatural serial killer.

I pretend not to hear him and dash out of the gates. Mr. Atkins shouts for me again, not hiding his annoyance. My legs forget all about being sore as I sprint up Coconut Hill. I stop at the top to catch my breath.

Mr. Atkins is at the bottom of the hill, but his expression isn't one of anger. He seems . . . wary? Maybe his facial muscles don't know how to show fear, so this expression is the closest thing to it. He is rooted to the spot; not even his large mustache moves in the wind. Then, Mr. Atkins hurries back to the school.

What was that about?

I turn around, and my heart skips a beat.

The monstrous silk cotton tree looms behind me.

In my eagerness to get away, I had dashed straight toward it, forgetting that it's a danger zone. The place always felt magical to me, until I found out it was actually magical . . . or, I should say, cursed.

But why would Mr. Atkins be afraid of the tree?

Then, it hits me.

Mariss was terrified of the silk cotton tree as well. If Mr. Atkins *is* the Heartman, maybe it was his prison too. Maybe he followed me up north *from* Fairy Vale.

Someone could have cut into the silk cotton tree and released him.

A strong breeze causes the branches to sway in a mocking dance. Goose bumps form on my skin as I lean to examine the trunk for marks. I don't dare go closer in case I trip on a root and accidentally scratch the tree.

There's nothing there, but the tree could have healed itself like it did last time.

I have to talk to Ahkai. He's the only person who will believe this theory.

Luckily, I spy the blue Transport Board bus coming up the hill, and the driver is nice enough to stop for me though I'm not at the bus stop.

A few minutes later, I hop off the bus and rush into Miss Mo's house. I head straight to the backyard, expecting to see Ahkai whittling away on the step or playing with Inkblot, but he's not there. I check his bedroom next.

I recognize Lynne's voice as I reach the top of the stairs. I press my back against the wall and inch closer to Ahkai's room, where there's a slight crack in the door.

"How do you put up with her?" she asks, her voice laced with disgust. Then a sound of her munching on chips or biscuits. *Does she ever stop eating?*

"You can trust her," Ahkai replies. "Just tell her."

"Not a chance. She's as spoiled and selfish as I expected. You deserve an award for sticking with her this long."

My hands shake with anger, but I resist barging into the room. I'm pretty sure she's talking about me, and I don't want her to know I'm eavesdropping. Instead, I wait for Ahkai to defend me.

He sighs. "Jo can be difficult, I know . . ."

I reel, as if someone slapped me. I would have preferred a punch over Ahkai's words. My head spins, consumed by the sting of his betrayal. An angry sob builds in my throat, one that would reveal my presence, so I hurry down the stairs, trying to hold it in as long as I can.

When I get outside, I furiously wipe away the tears from my eyes. Before Lynne showed up, no one would dare speak a bad word against Ahkai in front of me—not if they wanted to keep their tongue. I've never doubted Ahkai had my back, until this moment.

I don't know where to go. I don't want to be alone in my house—it's too dangerous, but I can't face Ahkai and Lynne, not yet.

Thankfully, Miss Mo pulls into the driveway. "Come help me with these bags," she says.

Ahkai comes downstairs to help us pack up the groceries, and Miss Mo provides a distraction by complaining about how much each food item costs now, compared to last week. Of course, she knows all about Coach Broomes thanks to her gossip network. Except in her story, he's not missing; he left his wife.

I take a long, hot shower that eases the soreness in my muscles but does nothing for the ache in my heart. Afterward, I pretend to take a nap on Miss Mo's plastic-covered burgundy sofa while she gets ready for some event at the church. But soon, the fatigue catches up to me, and I fall asleep for real.

Reeeekkkkkkkkkk.

My eyes fly open. *What the heck is that?*

It takes a moment to remember that I'm at Miss Mo's. It's dead quiet. She didn't bother to wake me but left on the tall lamp in the corner. The large painting of Jesus and his disciples at the Last Supper and the figurines in the antique cabinet, especially the giant ceramic fish, are eerie in the warm light.

I check my watch. It's almost midnight. *I wonder what woke—*

Reeeekkkkkkkkkkkkkkkk.

I sit up abruptly and whip my head around to the open louvers in the living room.

It's a chain, dragging along gravel. And not the light, clinking sound I heard in the cane fields. These chains sound *heavy*.

The rattling noise pierces the empty night as it clatters along the road. Goose bumps race up and down my arms as I wait to hear voices, a grunt, anything that sounds *alive*.

The noise stops, and I exhale in relief. Maybe a car broke down and is getting towed away.

Reeeekkkkkkkkkkkkkkkkkkkkkk.

The sound is closer, almost like it's coming up the driveway. I jump to my feet, planning to rush upstairs, but for some reason, I head to the louvers instead. I have to know what's outside. Clearly, I'm a glutton for punishment.

And I get exactly what I deserve . . .

In the middle of the driveway is a tall figure on top of a large animal.

The Heartman . . . riding the steel donkey.

Outside is dark, but the large moon is bright enough for me to make out a black wide-brimmed hat, pulled low over his face, and a dark cloak that swallows his body.

My hands start to shake, and my heart beats several times faster than its regular speed. I am too scared to move away. I don't even want to blink, in case he'd be right in front of me when I open my eyes.

Something shiny catches in the light at his side—another chain? No, it's either a long knife or a cutlass; whatever the weapon is, it's sharp enough to cut out hearts.

I want to touch it.

I press my face onto the louvers; I want to know if the blade is as sharp as it looks. All I have to do is open the front door and step outside.

Something knocks over the plastic bottles in the backyard, breaking me out of my trance. The steel donkey releases a puff of smoke that swirls and rises into the air. Then, two glowing red eyes appear on its face, floating in the circle of darkness.

Move now! my brain screams, reminding me that I didn't listen last time and found myself passed out under a windowsill.

The Heartman leans forward, his head stretching at an impossible angle, and it's only when his neck cracks in my direction that I find the courage to leap away from the window.

I slam the louvers shut and dash upstairs.

CHAPTER 12

I can't afford to keep a grudge against one of the few people who may believe that the Heartman is real. I barrel into Ahkai's room, tripping over a shoe on the floor and head straight to the lump under the covers.

Then, on second thought, I pivot to his bedroom window and slam it shut, in case I get another uncontrollable urge to go outside. The noise startles Ahkai awake, and he turns on the lamp on his bedside table, confused and groggy.

"Look! Look!" I shove his glasses onto his face and push him toward the window.

"What? What is so important?" Ahkai groans, adjusting his glasses.

I check over his shoulder and have to stretch my neck

to see the driveway, but even from this angle I can tell the Heartman is no longer there. I pull across the curtain and exhale with relief. I try to calm down, but somehow I've forgotten how to breathe.

Ahkai puts a hand in the middle of my back and guides me to the bed. It's full with books and clothing. I always tease him about his messy room; his rice can't touch his peas and his milk needs to be separate from his cereal, but it's okay for his room to resemble the aftermath of a hurricane.

After taking several deep breaths, I tell him everything. About the chains in the cane field. Casper's story. The Heartman appearances. I start to pace, the movement helping my mind to focus, and give as much detail as I can. Although Ahkai knows the supernatural exists, he's still extremely factual and scientific, and I have no proof of anything. It's my word against logic.

I finish and hold my breath, waiting for his reaction.

Ahkai stares at me with a bland expression for a few seconds and blinks five times. "Juliette Charlie." Ahkai says my code name in a solemn voice. "Our new mission is to proceed to the school library tomorrow. We need to find out more about the Heartman."

I exhale and fall back onto the pillows in relief.

Despite what he told Lynne, Ahkai still cares enough to have my back.

"I will stay up," he says, grabbing a book from the bottom of his bed. "Just in case anything else happens."

I'm safe tonight.

A tear escapes and slides into my ear.

"Thank you, Alpha Mike," I whisper, before closing my eyes.

It seems like only minutes, but when Ahkai shakes me awake, the neighborhood rooster has already made its way down the street, its distant crows in the air.

"The library should be open now," he tells me. "Mrs. Edgecombe is doing stocktaking."

It's the first day of summer vacation and our street is full of life; cars beeping at neighbors as they drive by, birds chirping, dogs barking, and children's laughter floating on the wind. You can be happy and carefree when you don't know the Heartman is actually lurking outside at night.

I get ready in the bathroom and then peer into the hallway for Lynne. She's staying in Miss Mo's "everything room," the place where she keeps everything that can't fit anywhere else in the house. We've managed to avoid each other since I arrived, with her "feeling unwell" and eating dinner in her room yesterday.

No complaints from me. I don't want to force my *spoiled and selfish* presence on her.

Miss Mo is sorting laundry in the kitchen, on the phone as usual. Ahkai shovels spoonfuls of dry cereal in his mouth and shoots a look of annoyance at his mother. I bet she's forcing him to eat before leaving home.

"Hold on, Marva, I getting a beep. Hello?" Miss Mo says, and then. "Hello? Vincent! Vincent, that's you?"

It's my daddy!

I gasp and meet Ahkai's eyes. *Daddy would believe us!* I hate to ruin the cruise, but these are extreme circumstances. I rush over and try to grab the phone from Miss Mo.

"Yea, everything good over here. Wunna all right? How the toilets does flush on the boat?" Miss Mo moves the receiver out of my reach and raises her voice. "Vincent? Vincent? Yea, I ask where the pee does go."

I start to pull off the clothespins clipped onto her dress to annoy her. It works.

"Look look, here is Jo fuh you."

She sucks her teeth and gives me the phone, and heads outside to hang out the laundry.

"Daddy?"

"Bean!"

The only thing louder than the gust of wind in the

phone are the steelpans playing "Feeling Hot Hot Hot" in the background. "Yuh good, sweetheart? We in Bequia!"

"Dad, Dad," I reply urgently. "Listen, I saw the Heartman, with my own two eyes."

"Ice? Yes, nuff nuff ice here, and everything free. Tell she, Rori!"

Miss Alleyne shouts something in the background, but the connection is terrible.

"Not ice, eyes! Daddy, the Heartman is after me. You need to come home. Can you hear me?!"

"Me can't 'ear nothing," Daddy says to Miss Alleyne, before the phone cuts out.

I stare at the phone for a few seconds before hanging up. I shake my head at Ahkai. "It's just me and you for now."

Ahkai suddenly avoids my eyes and taps his fingers on the table, one at a time. Then he starts to rock in the chair.

"Spill it," I demand.

He sighs. "We should tell Lynne."

"NO!"

The word is out of my mouth before he can finish saying her name. Anger rushes through me as I remember his betrayal. Now I understand the guilty look on his face. But Ahkai doesn't know I'm aware he was bad-talking me with Lynne.

"She can help," he insists.

"Help? Help how? By making fun of me? I can hear her now." I mimic Lynne's flat, dreary voice. "The Heartman on a steel donkey and not driving a hearse? Well, gas is toxic, so at least he's environmentally conscious. Ta ha ha ha ha ha!"

I have to make up a high, hoity-toity laugh since I've never heard her laugh before.

Ahkai shakes his head. "She will believe you."

"Why, Ahkai?" I grip the chair, barely containing my fury. "Why would she suddenly believe the Heartman is real?"

"Jo—"

"No!" I cut him off. "If you tell her, I will never forgive you."

Ahkai's face twitches, and he doesn't reply but rocks so hard in the chair that it scrapes the floor. He's stressed out. Any other time I would compromise or meet him halfway, but not this time. He has to make a choice: me or Lynne.

Ahkai pauses mid-rock and then jumps to his feet and walks out the kitchen door. I follow him, and we don't say a word to each other the entire way to the school.

With no kids around, there's nothing to draw the attention away from Fairy Vale Academy's dilapidated exterior. It is seriously creepy walking through the corridor, with only the echo of scuttling insects in the walls. As we get near the library, a loud cackle brings some life to the building.

Ahkai claims the library is open for stocktaking, but I bet the librarian, Mrs. Edgecombe, just wants to read in peace without students bothering her to check out books.

I was right. We find her on the floor, huddled under a blanket, still chuckling at something in the book in her hand.

She notices Ahkai first, and her smile widens for her favorite student, but then she spots me and the joy melts into horror.

"Ma'am—"

She scrambles away so fast she could have left some of the gel in her Jheri curls behind.

No one knows about Mariss's real identity, except me, Daddy, Ahkai, and Casper. But if I had to add another person to the list, it would be Mrs. Edgecombe. She's an expert on all things folklore, but she's been giving me the silent treatment since last year, after Mariss waltzed into the library and warned her against sharing her knowledge with me.

I sigh and turn to Ahkai. "You're gonna have to do the talking."

Ahkai arches an eyebrow and folds his arms.

"You've spoken to her before! I heard you!"

"It does not mean I want to do it now."

I growl under my breath and then we follow Mrs. Edgecombe through the aisle.

"Ma'am? Ma'am?"

She ignores me and shoves books onto the shelves in a most disorderly fashion.

Normally, Mrs. Edgecombe is the loudest person in the library, forcing students to find a quieter place to study, but right now she's as quiet as a cricket with a leg cramp.

"We just want to know about the Heartman! Not *anyone* else."

That gives her pause. "The Heartman? Why?"

"Ummm . . ."

There's no way I'm going to tell her that he was outside my window last night. She would chase me from the library.

Finally, Ahkai decides to be useful. "For cultural preservation."

I don't know why it worked, but it did. Mrs. Edgecombe's face softens, and I take advantage, quickly summarizing everything I've heard about the Heartman.

Mrs. Edgecombe is impressed with my knowledge. "Well, there's not much else, except for the circumstances around Goodman."

"We know all about Goodman too," I reply, rolling my eyes.

"Really? Not many people are aware of the rumor that he was sacrificed by a society of Heartmen."

"Wait, what?!"

I am *not* ready for the possibility of more than one Heartman. Ahkai whips out a notebook and jots down the new information.

"Yes, a secret society of men who need sacrifices for their rituals to the devil. There's even a folk song about it." Mrs. Edgecombe clears her throat and sings.

> *Yuh better do good, as to do bad*
> *Yuh better do good, as to do bad*
> *Fuh they kill Goodman from Hillaby*
> *And they think nobody don't know*
> *Yuh better watch yuh step when you go*
> *down there*
> *And see that they don't kill you.*

That rhythm is way too sweet and lively for such chilling lyrics.

"Why?" I ask softly. "Why would anyone choose to work with the devil?"

"For wealth, of course. Money is the root of all evil."

Mr. Atkins has a big ol' house near the market! Miss Alleyne has this weird tendency to point out where teachers live, and at the time, I barely paid attention to the property. And what about his brand-new fancy car? It must be the most luxurious vehicle in Fairy Vale. How can he afford all this on a teacher's salary? It's not enough proof that he moonlights as a serial killer, but it's super suspicious.

"How do you stop a Heartman, ma'am?"

Mrs. Edgecombe scoffs. "Haven't you realized by now? Most legends just warn you to stay away."

I throw my hands up. "But he has to have *some* weakness!"

"I don't know . . . he only attacks after dark, so the best defense would be to stay indoors."

Our shoulders sag in disappointment. Ahkai and I had hoped the library would provide more answers. I can't spend the rest of my life afraid of the night and the monster in the shadows.

Mrs. Edgecombe hates to leave questions unanswered;

it goes against her nature as a librarian. "Maybe there's something in the *Treasure Chest of African and Caribbean Folklore* book, but I loaned the hardcover to another library. Ahkai, you can check the scans in the digital archive, but it will take days, maybe weeks, to get through them."

She's not exaggerating; even though Ahkai's a fast reader, the font is really tiny and there is no index. Ahkai nods and goes to the computer area, preparing for the long, daunting task ahead.

Another thought occurs to me. If the Heartman escaped from the silk cotton tree, there must be a way to send him back into it.

"One more thing, ma'am. How can you trap an evil spirit into a tree?"

The grave look on her face indicates I've gone too far. Mrs. Edgecombe resumes the silent treatment, folding her lips together so tightly they could crack a tooth, and hurries away.

I am determined to find out. It's the only reasonable plan so far, and it makes sense. Both Mr. Atkins and Mariss were terrified of that silk cotton tree; it has to be the solution to my problem.

Ahkai has four pages up on his computer screen at once. His eyes race across the tiny block text, only pausing on an illustration of an old man with a furry foot, surrounded by trees and animals.

While Ahkai reads the folklore book, I browse the internet for ways to trap evil spirits. It's *much* quicker than reading a book. In a few minutes, I discover you can trap demons in crystals. Maybe the same ritual will work for trees? I copy the spells into a notepad.

But how would I stop the Heartman from running away, or worse, attacking me while I chant the spell? I search some more. People on a flashy website, with ads popping up every two seconds, suggest a circle of salt to trap evil spirits in place. The technique had failed when I tried it with Mariss, but now I realize the mistake; I had used table salt instead of sea salt. Apparently, table salt is full of impurities and won't work against strong spirits.

All research suggests the best time to cast spells is at midnight during a full moon. *That was also when Mariss was most vulnerable!* The plan seems more credible by the second. I check the calendar: full moon is tomorrow. I can't afford to wait another month to get rid of the Heartman; if we're going to strike, it has to be soon.

Someone bangs on the door, startling both me and Ahkai out of our concentration. Clearly, they don't know how to act in a library.

"It's open!" yells Mrs. Edgecombe, and I roll my eyes. Neither does Mrs. Edgecombe.

Constable Cumberbatch and Constable Jones step inside, their faces so grim that the room instantly shrinks to half its size.

"Can I help you, officers?" Mrs. Edgecombe asks.

"Actually, we're here to speak to Josephine Cadogan," Constable Cumberbatch replies, his eyes on me.

"Is this about Coach Broomes?" I ask, getting more nervous.

Constable Cumberbatch glances at Constable Jones, who does something that makes my heart jump.

He removes his hat.

Bad news is coming.

"I am sorry to inform you, but . . ."

I stare at Constable Jones as he finishes the sentence, hearing the words but my brain needing extra time to process them. If I was on my feet I would have collapsed onto the floor.

Jared never came home from the party.

He is missing.

CHAPTER 13

I sit at Miss Mo's kitchen table, still in a daze and my stomach in knots. I can barely remember the ride back to Miss Mo's in the police car. Ahkai is next to me, his chair pulled close as if he's afraid I'll topple over.

It's one thing when an adult like Coach Broomes disappears, but the whole village goes on red alert for Jared.

Fairy Vale is officially under curfew.

No one but essential workers are allowed outside after 6:00 p.m.

Miss Mo does not have Miss Alleyne's way with words, so instead, she fusses with my hair and repeatedly asks if I'm hungry, but the mere mention of food makes me want to throw up.

For once, Miss Mo doesn't try to force anything down my throat. Instead, she puts a bowl of peanuts on the table and returns to barking orders into the phone and organizing volunteer teams. She suggests they ask fishermen to help the coast guard search the ocean, probably for . . . I can't complete the thought.

I knew there was a dangerous monster running rampant in the streets, and I did not warn Jared, not once.

As if he could hear my thoughts, Ahkai leans close to my ear and whispers, "This is not your fault."

He doesn't get it. If I had gone to Adam's party, or had figured out a plan to stop the Heartman earlier, Jared would be safe right now.

"I coming there now, Mr. Atkins, see you soon," Miss Mo says, and I stiffen in the chair.

Miss Mo grabs her car keys. "I going to the church."

"Why?" I ask sharply. "What's Mr. Atkins up to?"

Miss Mo rubs my back and totally misinterprets my concern. "Don't worry, I won't take long, two hours the most. Mr. Atkins leading the search team for the gullies and bushy areas. You know he got the military experience."

My hands fold into fists so tight my fingernails almost draw blood. The audacity of Mr. Atkins! But it's also very smart, since he could guide the search teams away from any evidence.

Miss Mo wags a finger in our faces. "Do not open this door for *nobody*, you hear me?"

As soon as the car starts, I jump to my feet and drag Ahkai upstairs. I check to make sure Lynne's door is still closed before stepping into Ahkai's room.

"We're going to search Mr. Atkins's house for evidence."

I change into sneakers and then start to throw any unnecessary items from my backpack.

"I don't know about this," Ahkai says, chewing on his bottom lip.

"Ahkai, please, he'll be busy at the church for the next few hours," I beg. "We just need some proof that he's the Heartman, maybe Coach Broomes's clipboard, anything."

Ahkai remains frozen by the door.

"Jared could be in there! Tomorrow may be too late for him. Please! Alpha Mike, I need you."

Ahkai sighs but then grabs a black baseball hat and sunglasses from his dresser.

"Thank you! You still have that tablet, right?" Ahkai nods. It was a birthday gift, but without the internet it's pretty useless, plus Ahkai prefers printed books. "We can record evidence with that, and the whittling knife, to pick any locks."

Ahkai comes over with a few items: a waterproof flashlight, Benjie's Balm, and a spray bottle—I recognize his homemade snake repellent.

All weapons we used against Mariss. I arch an eyebrow.

"Just in case," he says, dropping them in my backpack.

Finally, we're ready for Operation Smoking Gun . . . until we open the door and find Lynne waiting outside with her signature scowl. She's in another one of her ancient black dresses with an even bigger collar. Her skin is paler than usual, with dark shadows under her eyes. I thought she was just avoiding me, but she really seems sick.

"This is a bad idea," she says, folding her arms.

"You eavesdropper!" I exclaim, with enough outrage that no one would guess I did the same thing yesterday.

"There's a kidnapper on the loose," Lynne says to Ahkai, ignoring my existence. "And your mother said not to leave home."

She's not too sick to ruin my well-laid plans. "Please, Ahkai, we don't have much time."

Ahkai switches his gaze between me and Lynne and

shakes like he's about to explode. Then he closes his eyes and jerks his head in my direction. It takes all my resolve to not yell "HA!" in Lynne's face. We leave her in boiling fury in the hallway.

I stop to grab a bag of sea salt from the kitchen before leaving, just in case.

By the time we make it to Mr. Atkins's house, we have a little more than an hour to find evidence and make it back to Miss Mo's. From the road the house seems glamorous, with its zigzag roof and wooden shutter windows, surrounded by giant palm trees. But as it comes into clearer view, you notice the peeling paint on the wood and large weeds overrunning the property.

There are no neighbors, and the land slants downhill into a gully. Someone could scream for days and only butterflies would hear them.

A bird squawks a warning, the cry echoing in the air.
We should have listened.

A large black dog pops out of the bushes and comes barreling toward us with a thundering bark that could set off a car alarm.

I yelp and start to run, but Ahkai doesn't move.

"Hello, gorgeous," he says, and the drooling man-eater's angry charge turns into a trot. Ahkai waits patiently as it sniffs him.

"Want a snack?" Ahkai reaches into his pocket and pulls out some peanuts. And just like that, the dog falls in love with Ahkai. After eating all the peanuts, it runs off to chase a chicken that had wandered out of the bushes.

"What is it with you and dangerous animals?" I grumble. Still, I let him through the rusty gate first, just in case Mr. Atkins has any ferocious pets for him to tame.

The wooden shutter windows at the front of the house are closed, preventing us from peeking inside. Plus, Mr. Atkins has the nerve to have one of those dead bolt locks that needs a combination on his front door.

"Let's go around back," I suggest. I listen for suspicious noises as we walk between several potted plants, trees, and elevated barrels.

Luckily, there's a small open window at the back of the house, near a rusty deep freezer. We'd just need to push the freezer across a few inches and climb on top of it to reach the window.

I lift the freezer lid to make sure it's empty and then gag, reeling away. Ahkai, curious about my reaction, peeks into the freezer before I can warn him and then slams it shut.

It is filled with thousands of long, pink wiggling worms.

"Oh God, what if Jared is under, is under . . ." I close

my eyes, trying to force the image of his decaying body from my mind.

There's no time to process this horror before another arrives—a car pulling up to the gate.

Mr. Atkins is home!

I grab Ahkai's hand and rush into nearby bushes, crouching low to the ground. Ahkai pants next to me, and I squeeze his hand, willing him to be quiet. My own heart is ready to leap from my chest, but I force myself to stay calm—we still need proof.

I slowly open the bag, the sound of the zipper cutting through the silence, and I hold my breath, expecting Mr. Atkins to yank us from our hiding place. After a few seconds, I am brave enough to remove the tablet, prop it up onto some branches above us, and set it to record. From our angle, we can see up to the middle of the deep freezer, so I hope the camera has a wider view.

Heavy footsteps crunch on gravel, and Mr. Atkins's shiny black boots come into view. He spends a few minutes dragging boxes aside, all while I do my best to keep still in the itchy bushes.

A car door slams and someone calls out, "Inside!"

Ahkai jerks next to me.

It's Miss Mo.

Mr. Atkins bends down, and we get a glimpse of the

hard, cold look on his face. He gets to his feet, and then a curved silver blade falls into view, the sunlight bouncing off its sharp, jagged edges.

Ahkai and I gasp.

"Helloooo?" Miss Mo calls, her voice closer.

He's going to cut out Miss Mo's heart right now. We'll have the attack on camera, but there's no way I can just sit back and let him hurt her.

Mr. Atkins pauses by the edge of the house, his gloved hand tightening around the handle as he lifts the blade higher.

"Stop!" I yell, and burst from the bushes. Ahkai jumps out, wielding an old boot as a weapon in one hand and the tablet in the other.

Miss Mo screams, and a cardboard box falls from her hands, and sweet potatoes roll across the grass. Mr. Atkins is taken by surprise too but still manages to control his swing, bringing the blade down into a stalk. A hand of ripe plantains drops to the ground.

"Josephine Elisabeth Zara Cadogan and Ahkai Anthony Moses." Miss Mo's eyes bulge in anger. "What wunna doing here in the bush?!" she shrieks.

Mr. Atkins's expression is unreadable, but he rests his blade on a brick and collects the plantains. "And trespassing on private property."

I stand there with a gaping mouth, my brain still catching up with the sight before me. I was supposed to be saving her from a bloodthirsty villain, but instead I'm facing two outraged adults, surrounded by vegetables. I glance at Ahkai, who is as flabbergasted as me. Then he hurries over to Miss Mo and whispers in her ear, and hitting the side of his neck. Whatever he says makes her even more upset.

"What am *I* doing here?" She places her hands on her hips. "I'm collecting provisions to cook for the volunteers. Now don't get me vex, what you doing on Mr. Atkins's farm?"

"Farm?" Now that I'm not focused on the house, I take in the numerous plantain and banana trees, and plowed garden rows around me. Until my eyes land on the freezer again. "Miss Mo, look in there!"

A flash of confusion comes across Mr. Atkins's face. "Something happen to my worm bin?"

He strides to the freezer, and I choke as he reaches inside. Mr. Atkins pulls out a fistful of worms in black soil, examines it, and then mixes it into a plant pot.

Fertilizer. I scratch at my arms, still unable to understand how I got everything so wrong.

"If I gotta ask a third time . . ." Miss Mo warns.

"I wanted to ask Mr. Atkins what would happen for

the cricket finals, if if if we don't find Jared," I blurt out.

Mr. Atkins sucks his teeth, long and hard. Miss Mo's face softens, but not by much. "Jo, I understand you worried, but I specifically told you all not to leave home. And, Ahkai, you should know better too."

"It's all right, Maureen," Mr. Atkins says, his mouth shifting into something close to a smile. "They already got their punishment."

I am confused until Mr. Atkins points at some furry brown pods in the bushes, where Ahkai and I were hiding.

Cow-itch!

Suddenly, I don't have enough hands to scratch the itchy places. My skin is on fire! Ahkai and I frantically claw at our clothes, but those prickly fibers have already made a home in our pores. As I scratch, my skin becomes red and swollen.

Miss Mo sighs and shakes her head. "I better get them home. Mr. Atkins, thanks for helping out at the fundraiser yesterday. Marva tell me that you was there the whole night, all after two in the morning, helping everybody clean up. Get some rest before yuh shift tonight, hear?"

Even in my itchy misery, the meaning of her words sinks in. Mr. Atkins was at the fundraiser all night. He couldn't have been outside the house at midnight. He has an alibi.

He isn't the Heartman.

Miss Mo berates us the entire way home, and Ahkai and I sulk and scratch ourselves in the back seat. "What were you thinking? Suppose the Fairy Vale Snatcher had kidnap you? And then Vincent would kill me. And then get lock up for murder! And then you and Ahkai would have to go live in an orphanage!"

She hustles us into the backyard to hose us down, still crafting scenarios where Ahkai's future children commit dastardly crimes because they didn't know their grandmother. Worst of all, Lynne comes down to watch with an enormous smirk and a "I told you so" in her eyes.

"Turn off the tap there, Lynne," Miss Mo calls, and then gathers up our soaked cow-itch clothing.

I rub my eyes, now sore from the water blasts. At least the burning itchiness has simmered down to a tolerable stinging. Ahkai glowers at me. A harsh soap scrubbing eased the irritation for me, but Ahkai's entire body is covered in a red rash. He's in for a long night of Miss Mo's awful homemade remedies.

Lynne takes her sweet time turning off the tap, and then the smirk drops from her face. She twists her hand on the faucet with force, as if she's trying to break it off.

But her fingers seem to be stuck on the pipe. How is that possible? Lynne jerks her hand upward . . . and the skin stretches from her palm like a piece of chewed gum.

I gape at her in shock, my stomach colliding with my toes. Her hand pops off the tap, leaving a slimy, transparent goo behind, similar to okra sludge sliding down a wooden spoon.

Lynne's eyes meet mine. At first she's alarmed, but then, she shrugs! As if it's normal for skin to be the same texture as melted cheese.

I can't believe it.

All this time I've been monitoring the outdoors, but the monster was inside the house with me.

CHAPTER 14

Pastor Williams always preaches, "Ask and you shall receive." Funny . . . I don't remember asking for monsters in my life.

I'm about to rupture my vocal cords with the loudest screech ever, when Ahkai covers my mouth with his hand.

"Don't," he whispers.

I almost choke swallowing the scream. My eyes dart from him and Lynne, and my brain clicks, putting two and two together.

Ahkai knows she's not human!

Inkblot races toward a puddle, and Lynne has to stop him from jumping into the dirty water. First Lynne's hand turns into a rubber band, and now a cat that loves water. I should have guessed she and that awful cat were in cahoots. But, is she working with the Heartman? Or is she the Heartman himself? When Mr. Atkins was a suspect, I assumed the Heartman had the power to change appearances, so maybe the Heartman can turn himself into an unpleasant eleven-year-old girl.

"I'll explain everything later," Ahkai says, before Miss Mo hustles us inside to dry and get some hot food in our bellies before we catch colds. At the kitchen table, she spreads a paste made of aloe mixed with herbs that smell like garlic breath on Ahkai's face.

I narrow my eyes as Lynne consumes a giant plate of macaroni pie and fried marlin. *Where is she putting all this food?* I bet she has four stomachs, like a cow.

Maybe she's not the Heartman but the steel donkey. I was so focused on learning about the Heartman I didn't ask Mrs. Edgecombe anything about the cursed animal at all. But Lynne definitely has the right personality for a four-legged creature. I can imagine her riding off into the night, braying Latin.

I glance at Miss Mo, waiting for her to realize that amount of food isn't normal for anyone, much less an eleven-year-old "girl." But now she's busy tending to several pots on the stove, preparing meals for the volunteers.

As the sunlight dwindles, every streetlight comes on, and so many cars meander down the road it looks like a parade. The volunteers, geared up in hats, backpacks, and flashlights, huddle in small groups in the streets.

My throat closes up, and I can't stomach another bite. Here I am, potentially sitting at the table with the creature that kidnapped him. A wave of disgust washes over me, and my nose starts to burn. I leap from the table and rush to Ahkai's room and burst into tears.

About a half hour later, Ahkai enters and closes the door behind him.

I don't waste any time. "What do you know about this—this monster?"

His face twitches, cracking the dried goo on his face. Ahkai sits on the bed and exhales. "Monster is a bit of a stretch."

"Her skin is the stretch! Suppose the Heartman sent her to finish us off? *She* could be the Heartman!"

He shakes his head. "Lynne has a good heart."

"A good heart!" I yell, and Ahkai flinches. "You've barely known her a week. What do you know about her heart?"

Ahkai bites his lip. "Actually, we have been friends for several weeks now."

Several weeks! Friends?! I recoil at the news.

There's no way—I would have known if he was hanging out with someone else. He sees the question in my eyes.

"Mainly when you were at cricket," he admits.

All those times I invited him to my matches, I thought he didn't come because he wasn't a cricket fan. I was trying to be understanding, less selfish, not letting him know his absence bothered me, and instead he was out with Lynne. Did Miss Mo know about this friendship too? Did they sneak Lynne out the back garden when they saw me arriving home?

"What kind of monster is she?" I demand in fury.

"Stop calling her that." Ahkai looks absolutely miserable, but I'm too upset to care. "It's not my secret to tell."

I tilt my head and open my eyes to the fullest, urging him to break.

"It's not my secret to tell," he repeats, avoiding my eyes.

"Ahkai, Mariss and her snake children nearly killed us last year. Have you forgotten that? Howwwww—How are you just okay being friends with a person who—a thing—whatever she is! She is not human. She can't be trusted."

"Lynne is not Mariss," he says in a cold, hard voice.

Then his face settles into that vacant expression; I

won't get anything else out of him right now. I get off the bed with a huff and stomp to the bathroom, not because I had to go but because the room is suffocating with his betrayal.

I slam the door behind me and then stop short.

Lynne is about to go into her room, but she pauses and turns to me. Neither of us moves. I stare at her staring at me. Her scorching gaze burns though my brain, filling me with fear and unease. The large collar flaps around her shoulders, even though there's no wind in the hallway.

But none of this bothers me more than the new necklace around her neck.

It has a pendant. Almost identical to the hummingbird pendant Ahkai gave me for my birthday last year, except it's a carving of a sea turtle.

My breath catches in my throat as I inspect it, not believing the sight before my eyes.

Ahkai made a friendship necklace for Lynne.

We both touch the pendants Ahkai whittled for us at the same time. And then she smiles—not her usual close-lipped condescending smirk either. It's a wide, gaping grin that I'm sure will haunt me forever.

Because there are no teeth in her mouth.

I am screaming inside but still too shocked to release

anything but a choked breath. I gather enough wits to bolt into the bathroom, locking the door and then heaving against it. I experience an awful feeling of déjà vu; I'm trapped in a house with a monster, yet again.

And just like before, I'm not sure what kind of creature it is. Lynne could be one of the Heartman's minions, like the lionfish were to Mariss. Or she could be a new manifestation of the Heartman, and that dreaded black cat her sidekick. Maybe Inkblot really does have magical whiskers that can strangle you in your sleep.

How can Ahkai ignore the fact that people started to disappear as soon as she showed up? And he never keeps secrets from me. This isn't like him.

Then new understanding dawns on me.

This is not like Ahkai at all!

Lynne must have him under a spell, just like how the Heartman was able to tempt me to jump out a window. Just like Mariss did with Daddy.

Ahkai is bewitched!

Last time, Daddy had to find the inner strength to break free from Mariss's spell, when my life was in danger. Does this mean I have to put my life at risk to save Ahkai? There has to be another way to break Lynne's hold on him.

If Lynne is the Heartman, she must have escaped

from the silk cotton tree. Even if she's only his hench-man, I bet she came from the same place. I intend to send her right back into that silk cotton tree.

I sit on the toilet seat and gaze out the window.

The only person on our street now is Mr. Atkins, who drives his black Jeep so slowly down the road he might as well be on foot, shining a heavy-duty flashlight into every nook and cranny.

It is almost full moon. If I'm going to banish Lynne, I don't have a lot of time to do it.

For the next couple hours, I brainstorm a plan for Operation Take Out the Garbage a.k.a. Lynne.

CHAPTER 15

I wake up with a start, my neck stiff and throbbing. I fell asleep on the bathroom floor while brainstorming ways to get rid of Lynne. A bright line of burnt orange peeks out from the horizon; it's almost sunrise.

I check the hallway for Lynne and then hurry into Ahkai's room, but sleep doesn't come. Too many thoughts race through my brain: plans for Lynne, worry about Ahkai and Jared, concern for Coach Broomes, and the burden of having to deal with everything alone.

I give up on sleep and head downstairs for some ginger tea. Miss Mo is already in the kitchen, washing dishes.

She pauses and answers the question in my eyes with a sad shake of her head.

There's no update about Jared.

But on the table is today's newspaper, and a large photo of Jared's smiling face is on the front page. The picture was taken last year, after he'd won Man of the Match at a regional youth cricket meet in Antigua. Before I know it, I am sobbing in Miss Mo's apron. She squeezes me into her soft belly and rubs my head.

The phone rings. She maneuvers her body to answer, not letting me go.

"Vincent?"

Daddy! I stiffen in Miss Mo's arms, waiting to hear if the connection is clear.

"Listen, there's some trouble—oh, you know already. Uh-huh, uh-huh, yea, she right here."

Miss Mo gives me the receiver.

"Bean?"

His voice is so clear he could be right next to me. Tears pool in my eyes again.

"Daddy!"

"We hear the news, and we coming 'ome, okay? I organize a flight back for tomorrow."

Relief rushes through me, and I step away from Miss Mo, lowering my voice. "Daddy, something else escape from the silk cotton tree, the Heartman. I saw him."

There's silence, and then the sound of a door closing

echoes in the phone. I chew on my bottom lip, worried he won't believe me. "Daddy?"

"Listen, Bean, you are not to go anywhere by yourself, you 'ear me?" he replies, in a hushed voice. "In fact, don't leave the house. I gine try to reach back sooner. Lemme see if I can sort that out now. Love you, you 'ear what I say?"

I nod. "Okay. Love you too."

I hang up, feeling ten times better, until I spot the calendar on the wall.

Tonight is the last night for a full moon.

If I don't perform the ritual tonight, I may have to wait another month. I can't survive that, and neither will Ahkai or any other kid in Fairy Vale.

I have to test Operation Salt Trap today, to see if Lynne can escape the salt barrier. I still haven't figured out how to get her to the silk cotton tree, but I have to perform the ritual by midnight tonight. I have the binding spells from the internet—but who knows if they'll work?

Miss Mo puts a kettle on the stove, and I decide to take a risk.

"Miss Mo, you know of any binding spells? One that can trap evil spirits into crystals and . . . or other things."

Miss Mo goes still. "Why you want to know that, Josephine?"

Uh-oh, retreat!

"I was just wondering, but never mind."

Miss Mo hurries over and brings her face to mine, so close I smell the peppermint tea on her breath.

"Josephine, I don't want you messing around with no devil magic. That is dangerous dangerous dangerous! You don't know what evil you might accidentally release into the world."

I have to hold in my bark of laughter. I definitely know it.

"You still got the crystal I give you, right?"

I nod.

"That gine protect you from evil so you ain' got to worry about no spells. Leave well enough alone."

I guess the internet spells will have to do.

Miss Mo insists that we recite the Lord's Prayer five times. Then she pulls a vial of holy water from her bosom and sprinkles it everywhere, even under the table. "Go and wake up Ahkai and Lynne," she says. "Wunna could help put up some missing flyers."

I trudge up the stairs, already planning to wake Ahkai first, but then stop short. This is an opportunity to carry out Operation Salt Trap. I sneak back down to the kitchen and grab some sea salt while Miss Mo is busy sweeping.

Outside of Lynne's room, I sprinkle a thick line of crystals across the door. If it works, Lynne shouldn't be able to cross it.

I take a deep breath and knock on the door. It sways open as soon as my knuckles touch it. I hesitate but then take two steps inside.

My eyes have to adjust to the darkness, though the light from the hallway reveals how much Miss Mo's everything room has changed.

The room smells of a strange earthy scent. A stack of cardboard boxes block the window, and the vacuum, popcorn machine, and mismatched chairs are pushed to the farthest corner of the room. There's an inflatable bed on the floor but no sign of Lynne.

"Why are you here?"

I squeal and jump back, hitting into the door and slamming it shut. Now inside the room is pitch-black. Before I can react, there's a tiny click, and a yellow lamp brings a soft glow to the room. Now I see the source of the earth scent; a whole side of the room is full of rocks, shells, potted plants of various sizes, and even a small pile of soil in the corner. How is Miss Mo okay with dirt in her house?!

And I still don't see Lynne, not until she pops her head from the sheet. It's a thick, black velvet material, which blends perfectly with the sofa bed.

She scowls at me and sits up. "You know, I stay in here so I don't have to see your face."

"Miss Mo wants you to come down for breakfast." I turn away, in a hurry to leave the room.

"Any news about Jared?" Lynne asks.

I swing around. I don't like the sound of his name on her lips at all. "What did you do to him?"

Lynne rolls her eyes. "This is what I get for being nice."

I step closer. "You better not have hurt him. Jared's my—um—he's my—er, I haven't figured it out yet, but I'm gonna take you out if you don't bring him back."

Lynne leaps from the bed, her face flushed and angry. "You know what? Stay away from Ahkai, before you get him in more trouble."

I am so shocked I start to splutter. "Me? *Me?*"

"Yes, you. *You!*" She jabs a finger in my face. "Clearly bad things happen to people who like you."

Something snaps inside of me. The crack echoes in my head as I'm overcome by fear and hurt, and then comes the rage.

Without thinking, I push Lynne's chest in anger,

channeling all the anxiety and angst from the last few days into that shove.

It's like I slammed into a wall of broken glass.

For a second I'm stunned, and then the pain kicks in. It feels like I ran my hands across a sharp grater. I make a strangled sound in my throat, and my eyes start to water. I spread my fingers, fully expecting the flesh to be gone. It's still intact, though my palms are red.

Lynne smirks at me in her crude, mocking way. Her teeth are back. "You're so weak. How do you expect to protect your friends when you can barely defend yourself?"

The pain in my hands has already lessened to a tingle, but my skin becomes numb, like I walked into a freezer.

Lynne has finally showed her true colors. And she's as dangerous as I thought. I shouldn't be alone with her.

I hurry to the door before my legs stop working.

"Wait!" Lynne calls behind me. "You're bleeding."

What did she do to me?

In the hallway, I pause long enough to see if Lynne can cross the salt barrier. She's in the doorway, staring down at the line of sea salt. Then she steps back into her room and slams the door.

Operation Salt Trap is a success! The sea salt works!

Then Miss Mo appears at the top of the stairs with

her broom. She mutters under her breath, and before I can stop her, she bends down and sweeps away the line of salt.

As she's getting to her feet, Miss Mo glances at me and drops the dustpan.

"Jo, yuh bleeding," she whispers.

"Huh?" I look at my hands. They're still red, but there's no blood.

Miss gestures with her chin, down at my yellow shorts, and I gasp.

I just got my period.

CHAPTER 16

Apparently I'm a new Josephine now.

New Josephine had to sit through a long, embarrassing talk about how to properly bathe her private parts, as if Old Josephine had been showering the wrong way all her life.

New Josephine can't have fried chicken and chips for lunch but must instead eat stewed mackerel, sweet potato, and vegetables to "build up her immunity."

New Josephine can't go outside and practice bowling, though waiting in the house for news about Jared or an update from her dad is driving her mad. She must sit down and "rest herself."

I spend the whole day tottering on edge, frustrated

with New Josephine. I finally lose my temper at dinner, when Miss Mo insists that I sleep with Lynne.

"No. No way. Not doing it!"

My voice manages to be clear, though my entire body is shaking in the chair. With anger, and mostly fear. It was hard enough to sleep with a monster outside my door. How can I survive with one inside my bed? I clench the edge of the table to stay still, my nails digging into the wood.

"You're a young lady now," Miss Mo repeats, not changing her mind.

"I'm the same person I was yesterday!" I protest, but she doesn't care.

She starts to sing a hymn and leaves the kitchen.

There's no way I'm sleeping in the same bed as Lynne. I might as well camp out in the driveway and wait for the Heartman.

Lynne, who finished her lasagna in record time, promptly gets up from the table, a scowl swallowing her face, and marches upstairs with Inkblot trailing behind her.

I fume for a bit longer, but then a thought occurs to me. New Josephine might have brought a stroke of luck to Operation Take Out the Garbage a.k.a. Lynne.

Tonight is a full moon. I've got the sea salt for the trap and the spells from the internet to send Lynne back into the silk cotton tree—I only need to find a way to get her on Coconut Hill, and I might have better luck persuading her if we are in the same room. Maybe I could knock her out or tie her up when she's asleep?

I'm about to have another bite of mackerel when someone on the radio calls Jared's name.

My hand jerks, sending the fish flying onto the floor. I close my eyes, wanting to hear the news and yet dreading it.

But it's just a caller complaining about the curfew and runaway children.

I exhale and slouch in the chair.

"No news is good news," Ahkai says, avoiding my face.

I scoff. "That's a nice way to say 'at least they haven't found the body yet.'"

"I am serious. Have a little more faith."

"Faith?" I turn to him, aghast. "Since when does logical you believe in faith?"

"Actually, it is more fact than faith," he replies. "According to international statistics, ninety-nine point eight percent of missing children return home. Most are runaways—"

"Runaways?" I shout, and then lower my voice. "Jared wouldn't run away from Fairy Vale!"

"It is a slight possibility."

So much for him thinking with his own mind. How can he ignore the fact that Coach Broomes has disappeared too?

"Ahkai, this is Jared's home. He is cool, popular, and so so nice. Everyone loves him. And we have the cricket finals coming up too. No way he'd miss that. He wouldn't do this to the team, and especially to me."

Ahkai's eyes widen, and then he seems resigned, as if I confirmed something he suspected all along. "I see."

His expression goes blank, and he turns back to his plate.

"What does that mean?"

He's suddenly very interested in the design on his fork, but I stare at him until he responds.

"It was the day of the match against Gall Hill. Mum saw Pastor Williams outside the supermarket on our way there and talked to him for eighty-three minutes. By the time we got to your match it was over. You were walking off the field and laughing with Jared."

I rack my brain, but all I remember from the Gall Hill game was taking three wickets.

He continued. "I was expecting you to be upset with me, but you said nothing. I stopped coming, and you never brought it up at all. You were too busy with your new friends."

He said the last line with no emotion in his voice, but his shoulders grow tense.

"Of course I realized you stopped coming, but I was *trying* to be considerate!" I cried. "I know you aren't interested in cricket at all, and I didn't want to force you to come."

"It's okay, I don't mind sharing you." He finishes his last bite and pushes the plate away. "Everyone should know how awesome you are."

And that's all it takes for water to flood my eyes, and no biting of lips or anything could stop the tears from falling.

"You know you're my best-best-bestest friend, right?" I say. "And nothing can ever change that."

Ahkai nods and hands me a napkin. "Hundred percent fact."

I wipe the tears away. My Ahkai is still in there. Maybe I can break through to him with logic.

I gesture upstairs with my chin. "Does she have an alibi for the night Jared disappeared? And Coach Broomes? You have to admit it's strange that people start disappearing as soon as she shows up."

Ahkai frowns and then sighs. "I told you she has been in Fairy Vale for several weeks. You just happened to meet her when these strange occurrences began."

I make a face at the reminder that he and Lynne had been hanging out.

"Remember what I said when we first met?" says Ahkai. "When the hummingbird flew into the window and you thought it was dead?"

"Yes . . . you told me to trust you."

"Lynne is a good person. She didn't do it."

Ahkai would have sworn on a Bible if there was one nearby. He's so sure of Lynne's innocence. Maybe I should postpone the operation, in case he's right.

By the time Miss Mo sends us to bed, I still don't know what to do. Lynne could be innocent of the kidnappings, but she's still a monster, so there's no way I trust her enough to sleep next to her. And even if Lynne isn't the Heartman, suppose I delay my plans, piss her off, and then she transforms into some murderous creature before the next full moon?

After a visit to the bathroom, and one last desperate look at Ahkai's closed bedroom door, I squeeze the strap on my backpack and enter Lynne's room.

It is completely dark. I get on all fours and creep

across the room, cautiously patting the floor ahead until I find the inflatable bed. I check to make sure the side of the mattress is Lynne-free, and my fingers catch on something hard and rough.

Her skin!

Wait—no, it's a cardboard box.

Lynne has a row of boxes on the bed to divide the space. I am both relieved and annoyed. If anyone should be setting boundaries, it's me. And she didn't bother to leave me a pillow or sheet either.

I get onto the squeaky bed, my body as stiff as a cricket bat, and listen for Lynne's steady breathing. I don't hear a thing; does she even need to breathe? I'm still trying to decide if I should cancel the operation, when an unfamiliar pain tugs in my belly. Was something off with Miss Mo's fish?

The sharp cramp spreads lower in my stomach.

Not food poisoning . . . *period pains.*

I groan. *Not now.* And I left the hot-water bottle at home. I would ask Miss Mo if she has one, but she might make me swallow one of her awful homemade remedies. I shift on the bed, trying to find a more comfortable position, but the cramps get worse. So much for Operation Take Out the Garbage a.k.a. Lynne tonight.

My body made the final decision for me.

I grimace and turn on my stomach, hoping that it will ease the discomfort.

"Are you trying to burst the mattress?" Lynne asks, irritated.

I open my mouth to insult her, but a groan comes out instead.

She pushes one of the boxes across. "What is wrong with you?"

I don't reply, but I turn on my side to see if the position helps. It doesn't.

"I'm going to get Miss Mo."

"Wait!" I yelp, imagining bitter bush tea or aloe being shoved down my throat. "It's my stomach, okay? And I forgot my hot-water bottle. Miss Alleyne said it would help with, um, the monthly pains."

I wait for Lynne to say something mean, but she just replies, "Oh."

There's silence again, and after a few minutes, I shift onto my back, and then another position, and another. I might as well be a chicken in a rotisserie oven. I hope I don't have to go through this every month.

Lynne sighs. "I'm going to try something, or neither of us will get any sleep. Don't freak out."

I wish she hadn't said the last part because I immediately become anxious. I reach for the salt in my backpack, just in case.

Lynne rests a gentle hand on my belly. No claws or anything sharp, but I still stiffen. I barely resist the urge to pull away, imagining sticky goo oozing from her hand and trapping me onto the bed so I can't move. Or scream. Or breathe.

At first, nothing happens, but then her palm gets as warm as a piece of sweetbread fresh out the oven. Then, in the blink of an eye, it's as hot as a fresh cup of ginger tea.

"Is that enough? Or hotter?" she asks, after a few minutes.

"It's good!" I reply, before realizing it really *is* good, like the heat burned the cramps away. I still feel a slight tug in my belly, but it is much more tolerable.

"How much hotter can you go?" I ask, curious.

"I don't know. I've never done this before."

Never done this before? She could have turned me into a human potato chip.

"This is so weird." Her hand is like a hot stone. "*You* are so weird."

"Me? You're the one who's bleeding without an injury."

"That's natural, not weird!"

"And this is natural for me." Then under her breath she mutters, "Humans . . ."

I grow tense again at the reminder that she's not human—that she's a monster. I can't believe I'm in bed with a monster's fiery hand on my belly. I mutter a quick thanks and turn away.

We lay in silence for a minute, each waiting for the other to speak again. Lynne starts to run her fingers along the sheet.

"Why did you help me?" I finally ask.

She sighs. "Ahkai says we should be friends."

Guilt floods my entire body, and for the first time, I believe Lynne may actually be innocent. After all, I've no proof that she committed the crimes, other than her being a monster, of course. But none of these Caribbean folklore creatures are nice to humans for long . . .

Then a warm blue light fills the room.

"Oh no," Lynne moans, "not again."

I sit up, pushing the boxes away. Lynne has her hands over her face, but it's not enough to hide the blue circles on her cheeks.

Her freckles are glowing.

The blue dots I saw from my bedroom window. Just before I saw the Heartman!

I almost fell for her "we should be friends" propaganda.

I leap from the bed, grabbing my backpack.

"I don't know why this is happening," she groans, still clasping her cheeks. "I don't know how to stop it."

I back away from the bed, and my foot touches something hard and cold.

A rusty chain. Long enough to drag across pavement. Caught red-handed! I should scream right now. Get Miss Mo and Ahkai so they can see Lynne for the monster that she is.

Reeeekkkkkkkkkkkkkkkkkkkkkkkk.

Lynne sits up, her eyes wide with shock. Now that she's no longer hiding her face, the shadows from the blue lights dance along the wall. But the noise isn't coming from her—the rattling is outside the window.

I point a shaking finger at her. "You sent a signal to the steel donkey!"

I reach into my backpack for the sea salt. I can trap her in the room and make my escape.

She puts a finger to her lips, shushing me. As I move slowly toward the door, she tiptoes to the window, and peeps through the curtain.

This is how curiosity killed the cat. Instead of high-tailing it out of the room, I am desperate to know what is outside the window. For solid evidence. I pull the tablet from my backpack and hurry over to record the steel donkey.

But the street is empty, nothing except for the light from the full moon through the trees.

Reeeekkkkkkkkk.

This time the sound comes from underneath the windowsill. We both jump back, take a breath, and then peer outside again.

Nothing.

"Why can't anyone else hear it?" Lynne whispers.

It's true. You'd expect neighbors to be turning on porch lights and coming outside with weapons. Not even Ahkai and Miss Mo woke up to check on us.

"You tell me," I reply, my tone icy cold.

"I had nothing to do with this." Lynne scowls at me, and her glowing freckles get smaller, until the blue light disappears, leaving only the glimmer from the moon in the room.

I head to the door.

"Where are you going?" Lynne calls behind me.

"To tell Ahkai you're the Heartman and you summoned a steel donkey."

Lynne sighs in exasperation. "I don't know how to convince you that I didn't do anything!"

That's when a light bulb goes off in my head. I look out the window at the moon, half hidden behind the clouds. Pastor Williams said to "ask and you shall receive," so I decide to give it a try.

"Prove it," I demand.

Lynne furrows her eyebrows in confusion.

"There may be another suspect, but I have to investigate. Come with me."

"Right now?" Lynne hisses. "You get hit in the head with a cricket ball?"

"What?" I give her my best mocking smirk. "You scared?"

Jackpot. I hit the right nerve. Lynne bristles her shoulders and marches to the door, not even pausing to change out of her nightgown. She opens the door and steps aside, waiting for me to lead the way.

I have the sea salt, the spells, and, soon, Lynne at the silk cotton tree.

Operation Take Out the Garbage a.k.a. Lynne is a go.

CHAPTER 17

"This is a bad idea."

I shush Lynne as I creep down the stairs, careful not to fall and wake Miss Mo and Ahkai. Breaking my neck would be pretty terrible too.

"Now I know why your people are always in danger."

"Will you shut up!" I hiss, and then slap a hand over my mouth. The house is still. I relax and glare at her. "FYI, when you're sneaking out *you try to be quiet*."

"Excuse me for not reading the 'how to be an idiot without getting killed' guide."

I grind my teeth and count to ten. Good thing I'm getting rid of her tonight because I can't imagine another day in her presence. I check the time on my watch—over an hour until midnight. Plenty of time to get to the silk cotton tree. I'll be able to trick Lynne into the sea salt trap, banish her into the tree, and make it back to Miss Mo's before anyone realizes I left the house.

I unlock the kitchen door. The click seems extra loud and judgmental, as if it's saying, "Are you sure? There's still time to turn around."

I have to do this. For Jared. For Ahkai.

I turn the knob and pull the door, but there's some resistance. I look down and then nearly levitate when two yellow eyes stare back at me in the dark.

It's that darn cat. It settles against the door, pushing it shut. Lynne has to coax Inkblot away with a piece of fish skin.

"Let's go," I demand. With all this racket, it's a miracle that we've gotten this far without encountering anyone.

And that's when Mr. Atkins's black Jeep comes around the corner. Why is the whole world trying to stop me from getting to the tree?

"Back inside!"

Lynne huffs. "But you just said—"

I close the door, just as the Jeep passes by the house.

Mr. Atkins beams his powerful long-range flashlight through the kitchen window. The light moves away, then returns a few seconds later, this time remaining in place, as if Miss Mo might be holding Jared hostage under the kitchen sink.

It takes Mr. Atkins a whole six minutes to go away. Where was he when the steel donkey was under the window? I check the time again. Fifty-five minutes until midnight. Over ten minutes have passed and we haven't even left the house.

"Let's go." I take Lynne's hand and pull her outside, still calculating the travel time in my head. We can make it to the silk cotton tree in a half hour if we hurry.

Mr. Atkins's Jeep goes up the street, so I guide Lynne in the opposite direction. Then her palm starts to get warm again, and she moans, "Oh no."

Her blue, glowing cheeks light up the dark street, almost as bright as the screen at the drive-in cinema. Lynne claps her hands over her face, but it's too late. Mr. Atkins's car stops at the top of the road and starts to reverse.

"He's coming! This way!" I grab her hand and pull her through Miss Mo's garden, and the blue glow illuminates the bushes ahead. Something in the trees, hopefully a mongoose, scurries away. Lynne covers her face again, and I hold her by the hips and push her through the rows of okra like a shopping cart.

"Why can't you control your face?" I shout as I nearly trip on a tree root. How dare she make her abduction so difficult.

We hide behind a breadfruit tree.

"Seriously, you need to shut off your cheeks," I whisper. "Couldn't you ask your dad how—"

"I don't have a father." Lynne snaps, glaring at me.

"Or your mom—"

"I don't have anyone," she says, cutting me off again.

I grow quiet, feeling a twinge of pity. I would be terrified if I suddenly started to bleed and didn't know why and had no one to help me. Earlier tonight, Lynne soothed my stomach, and though I'm no supernatural electric heater, I press my hands against her cheeks.

Lynne starts in surprise, but then, she takes a deep breath and closes her eyes. She exhales, and, soon, her freckles return to normal. She opens her eyes and expresses her gratitude with a lip twitch. Then we cower behind a fence with overgrown weeds until the sound of Mr. Atkins's boots disappears.

Thirty minutes until midnight.

"We're going through there?" Lynne stops when the terrain changes from Miss Mo's plowed garden into wilder terrain.

"It's a shortcut," I say. And then, seeing the doubt on her face, "You scared?"

But this time the goading doesn't work as efficiently.

"There could be snakes hiding in the grass," she says, unable to keep the shiver of fear out of her voice. On cue, something rustles in the bushes.

"You're afraid of snakes?" Her confession catches me off guard. Somehow her having fears, the same one as me, makes her seem more . . . human?

Though it's dark, I can see the fear on Lynne's face.

"They can be really vicious."

"Come on, I dare you," I say, and this time she can't resist.

We trample through the bushes with nothing but odd bird noises keeping us company. Finally, we reach the park with the broken swings and monkey bars, and Lynne sighs in relief.

"Where exactly are we going?" she asks.

"We're almost there," I reply, avoiding the question. And then to distract her, "Cockfight tree!" I point at the tall tree with bright red flowers behind the monkey bars. The fiery blooms stand out in the darkness. I loved playing the cockfight game with the buds, but I haven't done it in years.

I explain to Lynne that the person to remove the most heads—the seeds—from the flower bud is the winner.

"I'm the queen of this game," I lie.

As expected, her eyes light up at the idea of competition, and we battle with the buds as we walk, making little quips when we win. I haven't had so much fun outside a cricket game in a long time. When we reach the silk cotton tree, I'm a little bit disappointed and full of regret.

The tree is even more menacing in the darkness. The night gets darker as we move under the bushy shade of the tree, near a convenient circle of moonlight that penetrates a space in the leaves. Lynne's still focused on twisting her flower bud, trying to get my seed removed, not noticing my half-hearted effort.

"I win!" she boasts, throwing a fist in the air in victory.

"No, you don't."

I pull the bag of sea salt from my backpack and quickly pour a circle around Lynne. She gasps and then takes a step back against the bark of the tree. I expect a reaction when she touches it—sparks to fly, her cheeks to glow, something, but the tree remains as dead as the night.

Lynne places her palm on the trunk, as if she can feel a heartbeat. "I know this place," she says in a soft voice.

"Then welcome home," I reply, my resolve rising. I'm not the villain—I'm just sending her back to where she belongs.

I grab my notebook full of spells and prepare to commence the ceremony.

Lynne turns to me in anger, her eyes bright with unshed tears. "I shouldn't have trusted you," she whispers.

"I-I'm sorry." My voice breaks. Right now, Lynne doesn't look like a monster but a scared little girl in a nightgown. All that's missing is a teddy bear clutched in her hands. But I don't have a choice. The kidnappings have to stop.

With a shaking hand, I flip open the notepad to recite the first spell—one I found on a message board from user bigbrother51 that seemed authentic enough with all the Latin words.

Lynne's eyes widen at something over my shoulders. My heart skips a beat. Did she call the steel donkey for backup? I turn around, and it's worse than I imagined.

Ahkai, in pajama bottoms and a faded T-shirt, is glaring at me. Not a regular upset stare either but real anger. He's never looked at me like this . . . ever, and it's all Lynne's fault, whether he's under her spell or not.

I gather up some fake outrage. "You followed us?!"

"I told you to trust me," he snaps. Then he shakes his head, and the anger in his eyes fades to disappointment.

"Why are you standing behind a circle of salt?" Ahkai asks Lynne. He's still staring at me, or rather, through me. It makes me feel like less than nothing.

"Ahkai, I can explain," I reach for his arm, feeling the need to be seen.

He steps around me, and I protest, thinking he's going to break the salt circle. But he stands outside of it and holds out his hand to Lynne.

"I can't," Lynne chokes. "It traps evil spirits."

Ahkai cocks his head. "So why are you afraid?"

"You don't know what I've done," she replies, biting her lip. "I am not ready to find out if it'll work on me or not."

"Trust yourself." Ahkai beckons to her with his outstretched palm. Lynne trembles and shifts her weight from one foot to the other, but then as she gazes at Ahkai, her expression changes from worried to hopeful.

Lynne takes a deep breath, closes her eyes, and steps outside the salt circle. I get tense, waiting on lightning to strike, or for her to explode into a million pieces.

Lynne opens one eye and looks down at her feet outside the circle. Then she squeals with excitement and throws her arms around Ahkai. He lets her hug him, and they celebrate, just like we did when we found out he was the top student on the island. Only this time, I am the intruder on their intimate moment.

I back away from them, swallowing the ball of hurt in my throat. I can't do anything about the guilt though, or the shame. Lynne is some kind of creature, but she's not an evil one.

Reeeeekkkkkkkkkkkkkkkkkkkkkkkkkkkkkk.

This time, there's the sound of galloping hoofs with the chains, like it's coming from under the ground. Suddenly, the tree comes alive, the leaves shaking around us. I finally, *finally* believe Lynne has nothing to do with the steel donkey from the utter fear on her face.

"Run!" Lynne shouts.

"Run *where*?" I yelp.

The hooves sound like a stampede, coming from every direction. Yet there's no vibration in the ground, no other movement apart from the trembling leaves. Ahkai, Lynne, and I swerve around, not sure which way to go. Down the hill toward home? Toward Fairy Vale school? I'm so scared I would jump off the cliff if I knew I could survive the fall.

Then a puff of hot air comes from above. A shadow blocks the circle of moonlight under the tree.

We exchange fearful glances with one another, and then look up.

The steel donkey's red glowing eyes meet ours. It bares its teeth, the muscles in its legs bulging like it's ready to jump and flatten us. The chain around its neck drags against a branch, making a very short and soft *reeeekkk*.

"No sudden movements," Lynne whispers out the side of her mouth.

Good thing, since I am paralyzed by fear. I couldn't run if I wanted to. The steel donkey blows hot air from its nostrils, so strong that the circle of salt disappears, escaping into the air and sea.

Someone takes my hand. *Lynne*. She tugs it, and we all take a tiny step backward. The steel donkey huffs but still doesn't move. It crouches on the branch, and in the new position, exposes a steel armor on its back with sharp spikes protruding from the sides.

Wait, not an armor, a saddle.

I sense him before I see him.

The Heartman in his cloak and wide-brimmed hat, still covering his face, emerges from the leaves like rainwater sliding from a branch. The heaviness in the air is ten times more stifling than the steel donkey's breath. My heart thumps so hard it hurts my chest; my nose and eyes start to burn, and I get the urge to curl up into a ball and cry. The shadow forms into a tall, slender figure and settles on top of the steel donkey. Then, without warning, the steel donkey leaps at us.

"Move!" Lynne screams.

I dive out of the way, instinctively tucking in my elbows and rolling to cushion the impact, just like I do on the cricket field. The contents spill from my open backpack; a flashlight, cricket ball, a bottle of snake repellent, Benjie's . . . and Miss Mo's quartz crystal.

"Jo, look out!" Ahkai shouts from a distance.

The steel donkey and the Heartman are headed my way. A squashed can comes flying out of nowhere and knocks the Heartman's hat clean from his head—or it would have if he had a head! The headless shadow continues to urge the steel donkey forward. I can't outrun them, and I have no weapons, nothing but Miss Mo's crystal. I hold it out in front of me for protection, and it glitters in the moonlight. My fate is in the hands of a woman who believes banana peels protect her house from evil.

The steel donkey rears up, its legs pedaling the air, and the Heartman seems to bend in two.

It worked!

But I can't celebrate for long.

The steel donkey spins around and heads to Ahkai, who had been running toward me. Ahkai yelps and trips in his attempt to change direction.

The next moments seem to happen in slow motion. Lynne and I scrambling to Ahkai, screaming his name. The fear in his eyes changing to a blank expression of acceptance. He believes he's going to die. The steel donkey snatches Ahkai by his faded T-shirt, his arms and legs dangling in the air, and rides up into the tree.

Time moves again when I grab the flashlight and shine the beam into the leaves, but there's no one there. The moon shifts from behind a cloud, and a circle of light falls on me and Lynne under the silk cotton tree.

Ahkai is gone.

CHAPTER 18

Miss Mo sits at the kitchen table in her flower-print nightie and head full of curlers, confused, as a distraught Lynne and I shout over each other.

Our journey back to Miss Mo's is a blur; my feet were powered by panic. My chest hurts, and I have to remind myself to breathe. I am fuming inside: at Lynne for showing up in our lives, at Ahkai for following us to the tree, but I'm mostly angry at myself. I should have never left Miss Mo's house. Daddy warned me, and I didn't listen. He will never let me out of his sight again.

At some point, I stop explaining the situation to Miss Mo and just keep repeating, "This is all my fault, this is all my fault." It's a lot for Miss Mo to digest, but her dazed expression quickly changes to alarm when I hold up Ahkai's broken Simba cat pendant. Lynne and I fall silent as she reaches for the pendant with a trembling hand. Miss Mo pauses and closes her eyes. She clenches her fists and presses them against the side of her head. Then, her entire body begins to shake.

I brace myself for her explosion. Ahkai is my best friend, but he's her only child. I can't begin to imagine her pain and worry.

Miss Mo jumps from the table, marches to the phone, and punches in a number.

"Yes, police!" she barks. "This is Miss Mo. The Fairy Vale Snatcher took my chile. Yes, come quick."

Miss Mo hangs up and then passes out flat on her face.

By the time she regains consciousness, the house is full of police and neighbors. Miss Mo immediately starts to wail, and then pray, and then some jumbled combination of the two. Lynne, now in her black sailor dress with the big collar, sits at the table with a bowed head while I watch helplessly with swollen, bloodshot eyes.

Of course Constable Cumberbatch and Constable Jones don't believe me when I tell them about the steel donkey and the Heartman. Lynne lifts her head long enough to confirm I am telling the truth, but they're still skeptical.

"You mean you saw a horse?" Constable Cumberbatch asks, his eyes hard and cold.

"I know the difference between a horse and a steel donkey," I insist.

The constables exchange glances, and they don't write anything in their notepads. "Describe the man again."

"I told you, we didn't see his face. He was a shadow. Very tall and wearing a black cloak."

"So he was tall." Constable Cumberbatch scribbles in his notepad. "And dark-skinned."

I bang my hand on the table. "No! He was a shadow!"

We go around and around in circles, until I accept they have no intention of reporting the truth. Tired and worn out, I finally agree that Ahkai was taken by a tall, dark man on a big horse.

I am numb. I have no tears left, and the hole in my chest is so large I can disappear inside it.

Outside is a familiar scene, with police car lights flashing, vehicles parked on the sidewalk, and volunteers getting ready to search the area. A news van pulls up and blocks the road, causing the surrounding cars to honk in annoyance.

I observe all the chaos in exhaustion. They won't find Ahkai, Jared, or Coach Broomes because they refuse to see the truth. No one here believes folklore creatures actually exist.

Except one person.

I tap Lynne on the leg. "We have to talk to Mrs. Edgecombe, the librarian," I whisper. "She'll believe us."

Lynne shifts her foot away and glares at me. It's the first time she's acknowledged me since we arrived back at Miss Mo's. Then she looks around the kitchen. "Where is she?"

"Not here. She lives about ten minutes away." *Thank you, Miss Alleyne.*

"You can't possibly think I would go anywhere with you again," Lynne says, her voice filled with disgust.

"I'm serious. Ahkai is her favorite student. I know she'll help us."

"Us? Us? You gotta be talking to someone else." Lynne looks around the kitchen again for the mysterious some-one else. "Oh wait, you don't have any friends left. If you want to go get yourself killed, do it without me." Then she turns away.

The barb hurt, because it's the truth. Ahkai is gone, and it is all my fault.

This is why I have to save him.

I shoot out of the chair, my backpack clenched in my

hand, and slip outside. No one pays me attention in the chaos.

The streets are lit so brightly it looks like daytime, even though it's one in the morning. I sneak past gossiping, angry, and crying neighbors, until the crowd thins and the whispers of the night grow louder. A garbage bin bangs onto the pavement, scaring at least five years off my life. I reach into my pocket and take out my crystal in case the steel donkey makes another appearance.

"Oh Gawd, oh Gawd, why oh why!"

It's Mrs. Edgecombe's wail; I would recognize it anywhere. Ahead is her wooden house surrounded by hibiscus bushes. With its pink, yellow, and green trimmings, it might as well be the house made of candy from *Hansel and Gretel*. Her bedroom light is on, and from the street I can see her sitting by the window in a head tie. I barely recognize her without the river of Jheri curls down her shoulders.

"Lord, come for your world," she cries, wiping her eyes.

She must have just heard the news. My stomach churns, knowing I have to confess to my part in Ahkai's capture.

"Ma'am." It comes out like a croak. I try again. "Ma'am."

Mrs. Edgecombe pushes her head out the window

and furiously wipes her tears away. "Josephine? You got some nerve though!"

I drop my head. "You heard about Ahkai."

"Ahkai? He here with you? What you doing at my house at this time of night?" she demands.

Huh? When Mrs. Edgecombe leans farther out the window to scowl at me, the book in her hand becomes visible. She hadn't heard about Ahkai at all. Those tears belong to a made-up story. If I remembered how to laugh, I would. I wish my life wasn't real right now too, that I could turn the pages of tonight and wake up tomorrow knowing none of these events actually happened.

"Josephine Cadogan," Mrs. Edgecombe warns, snapping me out of my sorrow.

"The Heartman kidnapped Ahkai!" I exclaim, and then burst into tears again as I pour my heart out to Mrs. Edgecombe. And I tell her everything too—about Lynne, and how I tried to send her back into the silk cotton tree. Mrs. Edgecombe gapes at me with frozen horror for the whole story, and when I'm done, her fingers shift to the top of the window, as if she's about to slam it closed in my face.

"Josephine, Josephine," she gasps, clutching her head. "That poor boy. You don't even know how much danger you put yourself in tonight."

"I don't know?" I repeat, in disbelief. "Ahkai is gone, and it's all my fault!"

She removes her thick black glasses and rubs her eyes. "No no, I mean trying to cast spells! All sorts of evil spirits could have entered your body. Any ol' person can't conjure magic! You need years of training; you need to have a clear mind, and *discipline*. And you . . ."

She doesn't have to finish. If there's one person who lacks discipline, it's me.

"And you don't want to be trapping spirits anyway, evil or not. All that does is let the energy fester and then they wreak havoc if they're released. How would you feel if someone just took away your freedom?"

I picture Lynne inside the silk cotton tree, crying and beating her rough hands against the bark. Years, maybe even decades from now, some innocent person could accidentally release her and she'd just be a ball of hate. She's not evil now, but she would be by then. A shudder runs through me. *Maybe that's what happened to Mariss . . .*

"Give me your spell book," she demands. I dig into my backpack and hand it over. She flips through the pages, muttering to herself.

"Did I—I?" The thought is so terrible I have to force

the words from my mouth. "Did I summon the Heartman and the steel donkey?"

Mrs. Edgecombe rolls her eyes. "All of this is nonsense; look, this one is just the days of the week in Latin. You can't believe everything you read on the internet." She tosses the notepad behind her and ignores the loud crash. "No no, somebody else had to cut into that tree."

"You know about the silk cotton tree?!" At first, it's good to hear someone else confirm it, but then comes the anger. We could have made a plan to stop someone else from cutting into the tree, and now it's too late. But I swallow my fury because I still need her help.

"We have to do something, ma'am; what do you know about the steel donkey?"

She sighs. "The local stories talk about the steel donkey throwing rocks on top of houses. Most people just avoid getting cursed. But"—Mrs. Edgecombe adjusts her glasses—"there *is* the rolling calf in Jamaica. It's a similar manifestation of the steel donkey—a bull with blazing red eyes and wrapped in chains. They say a rolling calf is the spirit of someone who led a devious life." She recites the information like Siri on the phone. "To evade a rolling calf, you can hold up a mirror at an angle that will force it to see the reflection of the moon. You can also try sticking a knife into the ground to prevent it from chasing you."

Why would a creature who is afraid of the moon stride around at night? And you'd think that sticking a knife into the steel donkey would work better than putting it in the ground.

"What about the crystal?" I ask, remembering how it reared backward. "Do you know why it worked?"

Mrs. Edgecombe shakes her head. "But you can also try dropping items as a distraction, since the rolling calf likes to count," she added.

"So I have to depend on the steel donkey liking math?" This is the kooky advice I'd expect from Miss Mo, not a respected teacher. I give her a skeptical look that Ahkai would be proud of.

Thinking about Ahkai's face brings about a wave of despair, and I want nothing more but to curl up under Mrs. Edgecombe's window and bawl like a baby. I take a deep breath to pull myself together. I can't let myself break right now.

"Ma'am, how do we get Ahkai back?" I ask. "And Jared. And Coach. The Heartman probably took them too."

"Josephine, I'm sorry to say this, but . . . it's no use. If the Heartman really kidnapped the boys and Coach

Broomes, he would have taken them to his lair. Before you ask, I don't know where it is." She pauses, and then her face crumples. "They may already be dead."

"They're not!" I press my forehead against the wall. I can't let myself believe that. "Maybe you could go to the police and tell—"

She gives a dry laugh. "Do you really think they would believe a word of this?"

"Ma'am, we can't give up. There has to be a way to find the Heartman's lair."

Her bottom lip quivers, like it does when she's trying to keep a secret.

"What is it?" I ask.

She shakes her head. "No, it's impossible."

"Tell me, pleeeeaaase, ma'am," I beg.

"Look, Josephine, *I* don't know where the Heartman's lair is, but I can only think of one person who may have that information."

I get excited and wait impatiently for her to give the name. Mrs. Edgecombe straightens her back, which never reverted to its hunched position since it was healed by . . .

Oh no.

"No," I whisper.

Mrs. Edgecombe gives me a knowing look.

"Not her."

"Mariss," she says, bowing her head.

I've woken up from one nightmare and found myself in another. Even if I could find her, it's unlikely that Mariss would help me.

Mrs. Edgecombe wipes a tear from her eye. "So you see, our best course of action is to try to prevent any further kidnappings. I'm sorry, Josephine, I truly am. Ahkai was . . . special."

"Don't refer to him in the past tense!" I snap, forgetting she's a teacher. But who cares about detention now. I take another deep breath and swallow my scream of frustration.

Mrs. Edgecombe looks down at me, her eyes full of pity. "Give me a minute to get dressed, and then I'll walk you back home."

"There has to be a way," I mutter to myself, and stare ahead at the hibiscus bushes. Last summer, Ahkai was crouching in the same bushes with a walkie-talkie, helping me execute an operation to get rid of one of Daddy's dates. It can't be the last time he helps me out with a mission, it just can't. I have to persuade Mariss to help me.

"How do I find her cave?" I ask myself. Maybe I can go to the sea, plunge my head under the water, and scream her name. Anything is worth a try.

There's a shift in the bushes in front of me, a sort of shiver through the leaves. A cluster of insects hovers by the hibiscus flowers, but they're way too small to cause the movement. My hand tightens on my backpack, and I get ready to run; the last time the leaves moved without wind, the Heartman and steel donkey burst out of them.

Then, before my very eyes, Lynne appears in front of me like magic. Her face is pale and lips trembling. The cluster of insects melt into her face—they're her freckles!

"How–How—" I splutter.

Lynne's expression changes from fear to determination, and she gazes at the full moon. "I know how to get to Mariss's cave."

"How?" This time I say it with a mixture of accusation and disbelief.

Her eyes meet mine. "Because she's my aunt."

CHAPTER 19

I make a strangled noise. "Your aunt?!"

"Ahkai didn't tell you?" Lynne gives me a perplexed look, as if I am the one who just melted out of the leaves. "I thought that's why you took me to the tree."

"Josephine?" Mrs. Edgecombe calls from the front door.

"Quick, let's go." Lynne grabs my hand, and I yank it away, flinching from her touch.

"She'll stop us from going after Ahkai," Lynne warns. Against all reservations, I follow her in a sprint down the road. At the junction, Lynne turns to the left, toward Fairy Vale school . . . and the sea.

This could be a trap. This most likely *is* a trap. Lynne is Mariss's niece! If I wasn't the one who planned

Operation Take Out the Garbage a.k.a. Lynne, I would have thought she arranged for the steel donkey to kidnap Ahkai.

But even as I think it, I know that's not true. There was genuine joy on her face when she stepped out of the salt circle and hugged Ahkai. She cares about him, and wants to get him back. But does this mean I can trust her?

Lynne finally slows down by the deserted rum shop, and I lean against the wall full of ripped flyers to catch my breath.

"Can't you just teleport us to the cave?" I ask, trying to catch my breath.

She furrows her eyebrows in confusion. "Teleport?"

"You just appeared in front me," I reply. "Unless you can turn invisible?"

Lynne flushes in embarrassment. "Sorta." She rests against a faded poster for a fizzy juice they must have stopped making before Daddy was born. A second later, she melts into the background, like she turned herself into a clump of clear jelly. It's only because I know she's there that I can see the outline of her face, everything faded but her freckles.

"Camouflage," she says, wriggling her nose. The

movement makes her freckles look like insects on the wall.

Wait. A. Minute.

"That was YOU!" I yell, shaking a finger at her freckles. "You were in the yard, that time with Inkblot." The same insects were above the sink when he was dangling in the air.

Lynne reappears, her face full of guilt.

"You did that on purpose! Made it look like the cat was floating. You were trying to freak me out!" And Inkblot is extra attached to Lynne, sticking with her even when Ahkai is in the room. "That dreaded cat is yours. *You* left him in the backyard."

She gives me a wry smile. "His name is actually Urchin, but I like Inkblot better."

"And the chain in your room!" The steel donkey's chains are way thicker and heavier than the one I heard at the picnic. "Was that you? In the cane fields up North Point?"

Lynne winces and bites her lips. Her silence answers the question.

She sighs and starts to walk away. "We don't have time for this."

My patience snaps. I sit on the makeshift domino

table, a piece of board balanced on a rusty steel drum, and fold my arms.

"I'm not moving until you tell me the truth."

Lynne stops, glances up at the moon again, and then takes a deep breath. "I am a sea spirit, and I came here for revenge."

I open my mouth to yell, *Aha!* I knew she was dangerous! But now it doesn't matter that I was right. There's no one here to gloat to about it.

"What kind of revenge? Mariss sent you to kill me?"

Lynne's eyes meet mine. "I wanted you to suffer."

It's tense for a few seconds. I move my hand inside my backpack, in case there's need for the whittling knife.

Then Lynne shrugs and looks away. "I observed you for a few weeks and decided the best way was to get between you and Ahkai. I told Ramona that Mariss sent me—"

"Ramona was in on this?!" I exclaim. I should have guessed. Ramona had been trying to get pregnant for years, then Mariss touched her belly for two seconds and now she has quintuplets. Of course she was working with Mariss.

"Relax, she didn't know my plans. It was just easy to meet Ahkai when he came over to her house."

"But Ahkai knew everything?"

Lynne nods. "I confessed that I came to drive you two apart, and you know what he said? That it won't work. That you were friends for life. You really don't know how lucky you are."

And just like that, my heart breaks. I close my eyes and fold my hands into fists, struggling to hold myself together. Ahkai didn't let a vengeful sea spirit drive us apart, yet I spent all this time worrying that something as simple as going to a different school would ruin our friendship. He believed in us, and I didn't.

I gaze at my hummingbird pendant and press it into my chest, as close as possible to my heart.

I have to get him back.

And Jared and Coach too.

"How are we going to persuade Mariss to tell us where the Heartman's lair is?" I ask.

"She'll want a gift."

Sea spirits like Mariss loved to be worshipped. Last year, I used flattery to persuade her to release Daddy, but I doubt words will help me this time around. And I don't own anything valuable.

Lynne seems to read my mind. "Not money or jewelry, she'll want something that's special to you."

"Well, she's not getting my daddy," I retort. "And she already has the only picture of Mum—" I pause. I know what I can offer. The thought of losing it makes my heart wrench in my chest and brings the sting of tears to my eyes, but I don't have a choice.

I take the silk handkerchief from my pocket. "This belonged to my mother. It's not much, but it means everything to me."

Lynne nods, and I slide off the table.

"Lead the way."

Bright stars dot the sky. The crickets are loud tonight, joined by the sounds of odd, squawking birds that I've never heard before, or maybe I'm now listening harder than usual.

"You know," Lynne says, breaking the silence between us. "Ahkai was really—he is—he wasn't what I expected from a human. The few times I encountered humans they threw garbage in the ocean and mistreated their animals. Terrible creatures."

"Not *all* humans are alike! You can't judge everyone from the actions of a select few." *Ugh!* My own hypocrisy leaves a bad taste in my mouth. I flush in shame. Hours ago I called her a monster, simply because she wasn't human.

Lynne takes the high road and doesn't call me out. "Ahkai discovered I wasn't human when a baby sea turtle stuck to my hand. I expected him to freak out, but he just waited until I could get it off. He didn't ask me anything or treat me any differently."

That's my Ahkai. Never judging others. Everyone, especially me, should be more like him.

Lynne touches her sea turtle pendant. "He said he and I can be friends too. He told me to trust you, you know." She narrows her eyes. "I thought he was a good judge of character, until I met you."

"Hey!" I stop in my tracks, highly offended.

"Um, didn't you try to trap me in a tree not too long ago?"

"Okay, fine." I continue walking.

We take the long path to the ocean, though we're in a hurry. We both want to avoid the silk cotton tree. I'm still armed with the protection crystal, and Lynne has her . . . pockets?

"What powers do you have? Can you put people in a trance like Mariss?" It would be super helpful if she could hypnotize the Heartman. "Are you a half snake too?"

"I hope not. I don't like snakes." Lynne shivers. "But it could happen . . . my lower half could be a snake or fish. I've never transformed, so I don't know." She gazes up at the moon nervously.

We hurry along, passing through the fish market, and head down to the section of the beach where the fisherfolk park their boats. The sea is calm tonight, unlike my stomach. I never thought I'd be back here at night, getting ready to venture into the ocean to meet Mariss again.

Daddy's fishing boat brings some comfort as soon as I lay eyes on her red-and-yellow finish. I touch the handkerchief in my pocket. *Joanne* always finds a way home—hopefully she'll work her magic again tonight.

Lynne seems more nervous than I am. She trembles whenever the tide crashes against the shore. We push *Joanne* to the edge of the water, and Lynne takes a running jump into the boat, the bottom of her dress barely touching the water.

"Which way?" I ask, trying to ignore the urge to return to shore.

Lynne points to the left, and I start the motor and push the tiller forward. Daddy would go berserk if he knew what I was up to. He instructed me not to leave home, and instead I'm on my way to our greatest enemy. Hopefully I'll make it back safely and have the chance to beg his forgiveness.

The waves are as smooth as ice. Despite the danger, I am surprisingly calm. Maybe it's the gentle sound of the boat cutting through the water, or that I'm not making the journey alone. Or maybe because this time, I know exactly what is waiting for me in the middle of the ocean.

Lynne moves away from the edge of the boat when water splashes over the rim.

"Isn't the sea your home?"

"The sea is a big place, Josephine, that's like saying 'the earth' is your home," she snaps. Then she regains her composure. "I don't want her to know I'm coming, not until the last minute."

It makes sense. Last time, Mariss created a tornado wave to pull Daddy and me beneath the ocean floor. A shiver of fear runs through my body at the memory; I'm in her domain, with no protection. Now I understand why Ahkai put weapons against Mariss in the backpack.

I reach into the bag for the Benjie's, remembering how much Mariss hated the smell. When I open the tube, Lynne wrinkles her nose, but she doesn't gag like Mariss did.

"Where were you when she kidnapped Daddy last year?"

Lynne exhales. "Who knows? I lose track of the different places. People never keep me for long."

Keep her? I wonder what that means. "What kind of sea spirit are you? Did Mariss take you from the silk cotton tree?"

"No," she says reluctantly. "I was born in the sea, hence the name, *sea* spirit and not *tree* spirit."

"Well, you said you had no one, but you have Mariss, don't you? Where's your mother?"

"She's dead."

"Oh." I grow silent. I've given the same answer countless times. I didn't want anyone's pity then, and I'm sure Lynne doesn't want mine now. Still, I feel the need to say something more.

"This boat is named after my mother, Joanne. I don't have many memories of her. She died when I was five."

"Mine died when I was a baby. All I know about her is that she was weak and a coward."

I inhale sharply and glance up at the sky, expecting lightning to strike Lynne for daring to speak ill of the dead, much less her mother.

I change the topic quickly. "What about your dad?"

"Might as well be dead."

Now I understand what she means by "keep her." Lynne is an orphan.

Before I can respond, Lynne exhales in annoyance. "Enough questions."

"I'm only trying to help!" I shout. "If you tell me everything, maybe we can figure out why your cheeks turn into glow sticks. Maybe they light up when you're being dishonest, like how Pinocchio's nose grows when he lies."

"What the heck is a Pinocchio?" Lynne screeches, and then flings her hands in the air. "This boat needs to go faster."

Before I can answer, her freckles start to glow. Lynne touches her face in panic. "Oh no, look what you did."

"Me?!"

Her cheeks warm the path ahead, revealing absolutely nothing in the distance except the full moon shimmering on the surface of the water, so it's extra scary when something jostles the boat from below.

"What is that?" I grip on to the side.

The thing bumps *Joanne* again, this time tilting the boat. I yelp and yank on the tiller, willing it to go faster. We both peer into the water; I expect to see Mariss's spitting eyes staring back at me.

Instead, blue dots appear underwater, one by one, until the surface lights up like a giant Christmas tree. My mouth drops in awe at the hundreds, no, probably thousands of glowing shrimp, crabs, lobsters, every kind of shellfish swim next to the boat. I bend the tiller to the left, and they anticipate my change of direction, as if we practiced a synchronized performance.

"Is this normal?" I glance at Lynne, whose eyes must

have grown twice the size. Apparently not. A silver fish leaps from the waves, straight at Lynne's face, and takes a quick nibble at her cheeks before hurtling itself back into the sea.

A line of silver fish rise out of the water and jump over the boat. A few of them fall out of sync to take a nip at Lynne's face.

"Ah! That tickles!" She waves the fish away.

"I guess the ocean missed you."

Her firm, thin lips curve into a large smile. "I missed it too." She raises her chin, inhaling the sea spray, and then she giggles and laughs. The dots on her cheeks glow as bright as the moonlight. She looks majestic, like a vibrant fairy out of a whimsical tale. In that moment, I understand why people worship sea spirits.

The giant wave comes out of nowhere and lashes the side of the boat, sending us airborne.

The force of the hit scatters all the fish, and the night plunges back into darkness. I pedal the air for what feels like an eternity, and when I start to fall, I instinctively tuck my body into a ball to cushion the impact . . . which works well on a cricket field but results in a painful belly flop in the ocean.

It might as well be a brick wall. The impact knocks the breath out of me, and water rushes through my nose.

The sea twists like a snake, ready to devour me whole, its watery teeth yanking my backpack away. I punch the ocean with my remaining strength, determined to fight until the very end.

A glowing blue light appears before me. I reach toward it, but then my vision becomes blurry.

One last bubble escapes from my mouth, and then, everything fades to black.

CHAPTER 20

Darkness ... darkness ... and then, yellow light.

"Josephine, are you dead?"

My eyes fly open at Lynne's solemn voice. Then, I turn to a side and vomit up a gallon of salt water.

Lynne makes a sound of disgust and scrambles away. When I finish hurling out my guts, I take in the surroundings. A gentle pool of water inside smooth, crystal-blue walls. Glistening white stalactites hover above me like teeth waiting on their cue to bite. The beehive-shaped stalagmites on the floor are even bigger than I remember.

I'm back.

I get to my knees, still catching my breath. The air is boiling in Mariss's cave, so hot that my skin is already dry, and my T-shirt and jeans feel cold on my body.

"What happened back there?" I swallow saliva, my throat still burning.

"I saved your life, that's what happened," Lynne says, biting her nail. "She isn't happy." Lynne glances toward the path of glowing stalagmites that, as I recall, leads down to larger pool with a giant rock in the center—Mariss's throne.

"I *told* you we have to be quiet when sneaking, and you hoot our arrival on a wave of shrimp!"

Her eyes spark with anger. "Who had the oldest, loudest boat on the beach?"

"Don't you dare insult *Joanne.*"

The bickering helps me to manage my fear as we walk through the pathway. The cave now separates into three round sections. Mariss must have hired a new decorator. Seaweed curtains fall over the entrances, each of them bordered with intricate sea fan art.

"I need to go to my room for a quick second," Lynne says.

"Go to your room?" I repeat incredulously. "You think we're here for study group?"

But I still follow her because, one, I'm curious; and, two, I'm not ready to face Mariss.

Lynne's room looks like an aquarium. Glass tanks are

built into the cave walls, with several types of coral moving inside them, from hard white stones to soft jelly-like organisms with tentacles. A thick layer of shells lines the bottom of the tanks.

Lynne peers into one of the tanks and then another. "This is my research. I hope to find better ways to protect the coral reefs. They're dying, if you didn't know. And all the creatures, the worms, barnacles, mollusks, shellfish will be vulnerable too."

"So you needed to check on coral?"

"Not that." With every tank she examines, Lynne's shoulders slump lower and lower. Finally, she sits on the floor and drops her head.

"What? What?" I ask, alarmed.

"Nothing, it was silly to hope." She straightens, her eyes dull and cold.

Then a white, lumpy circle floats up from behind some coral.

"Luna! You're alive!" Lynne cries. The circle floats to the top of the tank and then turns on a side, revealing a gaping mouth that can't seem to close. Lynne grabs some seaweed from a pile on the floor and has to flip the weird fish upright so that it can eat.

"I can't believe she fed her. She thinks all sunfish are useless." Lynne tries her best not to grin. "Auntie M especially hates Luna because she can't feed herself. Luna is just a little different, that's all. I don't expect you to understand."

But I do, more than she knows. I tell her about Mr. Pimples, my pet angelfish. I was devastated when I lost him and wouldn't wish that feeling on anyone.

"She *ate* your pet fish?" Lynne gapes in horror.

"Yup, you're lucky Luna is alive."

As if on cue, a high-pitched humming echoes throughout the cave.

Mariss's foreign tune.

Goose bumps rise up on my skin and march along my arms. I forgot how that foreign tune haunted my dreams. I've reached for Lynne's hand. Or maybe she reached for mine? Who knows, but she doesn't pull away.

"Let's get this over with." She leads me out of her room and through the middle entrance, and doesn't let go until Mariss comes into view.

Mariss sits on her giant rock in the middle of her blue-green pool, still humming her tune. A small spiral necklace hangs from her neck. She's in her favorite red-and-white cotton dress, which hugs her hips and then flows loosely around her legs.

Legs. Not a snake bottom.

Mariss runs a brass comb with jeweled stones through

her gigantic blond afro, observing herself in a mirror. There's no mocking smile and no snake bursting out of her chest. It's so disturbing how *normal* she looks, as if she's a model in an underwater fashion shoot and not a vengeful snakewoman.

Mariss still hasn't acknowledged us, though she knows we're here.

Lynne has to half lift, half drag me down the stairs. *Stairs?* Those weren't here before either. Last time, I dislocated my knee trying to scramble down the rocks to stop Daddy from entering her pool of poisonous lionfish. Speaking of which, a curious lionfish pokes its head out of the water to watch the confrontation.

Finally, finally, Mariss shifts her eyes from the mirror over to me and Lynne. Well, mainly Lynne. Her expression doesn't change as her gaze travels over Lynne, from top to bottom, inspecting every part of her body. I switch my gaze back and forth from Lynne to Mariss, looking for some resemblance, but there's none.

Lynne says in the tiniest voice, "Hello, Auntie M."

Suddenly, Mariss smashes the mirror down on the rock. Both Lynne and I jump, and I let out a whimper of fear.

"What were you thinking, Novalynne?" Mariss frowns, though no wrinkles appear on her perfect, plastic skin. "First you have a conniption when I give you a *very* gentle snake for your birthday, and then you run away from home?"

Run away? I gape at Lynne, who has her face to the ground. I thought Mariss had sent her niece to finish her dirty work, but Lynne was pulling the strings all along.

"It bit me, Auntie M!"

"Only because you scared it. If you would spend less time playing with rocks and useless bottom-feeders, you'd be more comfortable with snakes. Do you *want* to have a sunfish bottom? Do you want to be weak and foolish like your mother? Get yourself killed, just like her? You won't survive out there."

Lynne snaps her head up in defiance. "I can take care of myself! At least I did something instead of sitting around complaining about devious men and spoiled, ungrateful children."

Mariss inhales a sharp breath but keeps her temper in check. She saunters down the rock like she's on a runway. "And how did that work out, hmm? I heard you fell for a human."

It takes me a second to realize "fell for a human" is referring to Ahkai. Lynne and Ahkai.

Together.

I wrench my eyes away from Mariss and gape at Lynne. "You like *like* Ahkai?!"

Lynne turns to me. "No! He's my friend, just my friend." And then she sees the dark look on Mariss's face. "No! Not my friend, he's just, he's, he's—" She groans and covers her face. "I do not want to have this conversation right now."

She's right. The mention of Ahkai reminds me of the mission.

I summon the courage to ask Mariss about the Heartman's lair, but my voice fails when a slow smile spreads across her face. "Josie Sweets, I didn't see you there."

This is the Mariss I know, with that sickening sweet smirk full of dark promises.

"At least you did one thing right, Novalynne." Mariss claps, but Lynne doesn't join in; she remains at my side.

I expect Mariss to continue toward us through the pool, but she sits at the bottom of the rock and folds her legs. "Let me make my home more comfortable for you, Josie Sweets. I hope you realize this time you'll be staying for good, though not for long."

Mariss reaches behind the rock, and I brace myself for a flying snake, but what she pulls out is much, much worse.

It's the picture of my mum. The one she stole from the TV stand.

I step closer to the pool, my eyes roaming over Mum's face, trying to commit her laughing smile to memory. The gold frame is just as bright as the highlights in Mum's hair.

Mariss's smile becomes more sinister as tears roll down my cheeks. "Tears won't save you this time."

"Auntie—"

"You stay out of this!" Mariss snaps. She gives Lynne an acid look that would send anyone running, but Lynne stands her ground.

"Auntie, just hear her out."

Mariss seethes in disgust. "I can understand you liking the boy, but this whiny sack of bones?"

"Hey! You—*ugh*."

Lynne elbows me in the side. "Don't piss her off."

Lynne moves to the edge of the pool and dips her hand in the water. A few sulky lionfish swim up to her, but they don't attack. Lynne strokes their spiky, poisonous fins. "Please, Auntie M, the Heartman kidnapped Ahkai, and Jo is going after him."

Mariss is silent for a few seconds, staring at Lynne with her deadly pets, and then me.

"Mariss, please, just tell me how to get to his lair," I beg. "I brought you a gift."

I reach into my pocket and bring the handkerchief

to my cheek one last time before offering it to Mariss. "This belonged to my mother."

Mariss gets to her feet and starts to walk through the pool; it looks like she's gliding on the water. Her face doesn't display any emotion; I don't know whether she'll help me or kill me.

"It's all I have left of my mum," I continue, trying to persuade her. "You can add it to your collection. Please, just tell me where the lair is. The Heartman took Ahkai and Ja—other people I care about." No need to give Mariss another name for her Josephine hit list.

Mariss twists her hand, and the water in the pool follows the movement, swirling slowly in a circle, and then starts to bubble. I close my eyes, preparing for the worst.

There's a gentle tug on my hand, and when I open my eyes, I see the handkerchief in a bubble of water, floating toward Mariss. When it gets close, Mariss caresses the material with her finger, before guiding it to rest on top of Mum's picture frame.

"The entrance to the Heartman's lair is in Independence Square, in the city."

Breath rushes out of my mouth—I can't believe it worked.

"Look for the coat of arms, that's the key."

Mariss reaches into the bubbling pool and pulls out my backpack with a manicured finger.

"Hurry now, people don't last long with the Heartman."

All my instincts warn me that this was too easy. Mariss could be lying about the location of the lair, but I have to go to Independence Square and find out.

I ease close enough to snatch the backpack from her little finger, still wary. "Thank you, Mariss."

"And remember, step on a crack, break your mother's back."

What the heck does that mean? I'll worry about it after I get out of this wretched cave. I back away from her slowly, and then turn and sprint to the exit.

"And where are you going?"

I pause on the stairs, but Mariss isn't talking to me. Lynne had started to follow me out of the cave.

"I have to help; she's useless by herself," Lynne says, rolling her eyes.

I begin to protest, but it's true. I have no idea how to even get back to shore.

"Absolutely not. I forbid it."

For the first time, Mariss looks genuinely angry. Her eyes turn from brown to yellow. I know what's coming. I've seen this transformation before.

"I'm sorry, Auntie," Lynne says, and runs toward me.

"Novalynne!" Mariss screeches, and her eyes turn red. She rises high into the air as her lower half starts to transform into its snake bottom.

"Go go go!" Lynne shouts.

We race to the exit together, and a loud hiss echoes behind us. In a panic, I grab Ahkai's snake repellent from the backpack and empty the entire bottle around the exit and down the stairs. Mariss roars in anger and then gags when the smell of cinnamon and other chemicals reaches her sensitive nose.

The cave walls shake from Mariss's wrath, and odd gruff cries fill the air, followed by heavy banging. Lynne and I narrowly dodge a stalactite crashing to the floor. We reach the pool that leads back to the ocean, but it's no longer calm. The water spins like a tornado. I hesitate, not willing to get sucked below to the ocean floor again.

"Can you control the sea?" I ask Lynne.

She shakes her head, but then Mariss screeches her name again.

Lynne grabs my hand and we jump. As soon as we make contact with the swirling water, Lynne's skin turns mushy, sticking to mine like glue. *Gross!* But also convenient when the water tries to wrench us apart. We swim toward a small space in the rocks.

"Keep still when we go through the tunnel."

My eyes widen, and I would have pulled away if I could. Lynne can speak underwater!

"I can breathe in salt water," she confirms.

"Novalynne!" Mariss's scream is just as loud under the water, and sounds much much closer. She could be upon us in seconds.

The current suddenly changes direction, pulling us back toward the cave like bits of dirt caught in a vacuum. I flail and somehow end up on top of Lynne, and my arms and legs fasten to her back. We might as well be two sticky marshmallows, with Mariss waiting above to roast us both.

Lynne's freckles start to glow again. "How—How—What's happening?" she asks. Even if I could speak, I don't have any answers. I can barely understand what's happening with my own body, much less a sea spirit's.

Then, hundreds of silver fish with flat heads burst from the tunnel. They attach themselves under Lynne's body. The current is no match for the fish, who propel us through the water like a marine rocket.

We break the surface, and cold air blasts into my face. I inhale with a loud gasp.

We're flying! The silver fish paint the ocean with shimmering sparkles that dance on top of the water. The wind lashes at my face as I press myself onto Lynne. We both hoot and squeal in excitement. The fish hover in the air for a few more seconds before plummeting back into the ocean.

I hold my breath, but it's not long before we're airborne again, and we travel in and out of the water; Mariss's turbulence is a gentle splash against this speed. The shore approaches, and the fish toss us into the air, one last time. Lynne's skin gets firm, and my arms and legs detach from her body as we fall and then land flat on our backs on the sand.

We lay there for a minute, catching our breath, not saying a word.

I sit up and rub my eyes, and as my vision clears, a bony frame in khaki pants and shirt appears above me.

"C-Casper?"

"Well?" Casper asks, his eyes red and wild. "Did the vile vixen reveal the location of the Heartman's lair?"

CHAPTER 21

I gape at him. "How did you—"

A series of incidents connect in my brain. The flying can at the silk cotton tree. The falling garbage bin. The odd squawking bird noises. "Casper, have you been following us this whole time?"

"Indeed. A good zoologist never interferes with the natural habitat." Then he turns to Lynne. "Hello, clever chameleon."

"Uhhh . . ." Lynne glances at me, perplexed.

A wave crashes against the shore in anger, and Lynne leaps to her feet. "We need to get to Independence Square, and fast, before Auntie M catches us."

"I know a shortcut!" Casper sprints toward the fish market.

Lynne gives me a side-eye, concerned. "Should we follow him?"

"It's almost three a.m. and no buses are running. Casper's all we've got," I reply, trying not to get too disheartened.

We follow Casper through the market, and he brings us near the public bathrooms, peering out at the empty road.

"Shhhh," he whispers, "wait a minute . . . it's coming."

I use the opportunity to duck into the bathroom to take care of my needs. I return minutes later, to see Casper in the same position and Lynne tapping her feet with impatience. Then a loud rumble fills the air and bright headlights penetrate the darkness.

"Ah, here it is, right on time," Casper whispers.

The garbage truck parks in front of the bathroom, and a door slams. The driver whistles a popular soca tune and goes to relieve himself in a gap between the vendor stalls, though the toilets are *right* there.

Casper uses the opportunity to jump on the ledge at the back of the truck and grabs the bar at the side, just like the sanitation workers when they're preparing to haul the trash.

I glance at Lynne and shrug. "It's better than walking."

A few minutes later, I'm still in disbelief. Casper, Lynne, and I are holding on for dear life on the back of the garbage truck as it drives out of Fairy Vale and toward the city. The trash door is closed, but the foul smell lingers.

"Ride 'em, cowboy!" Casper hoots as the truck flies around a roundabout. Lynne tries to keep her bored expression but gives up and allows a small giggle to escape.

"You should laugh more often," I tell her, and the smile immediately slides off her face.

"What? It was a compliment! Unless you prefer to look like you swallowed a rotten egg."

Lynne blows out a long breath. "You know, you're really judgmental. Why are you so determined to go to Lamming when you fit right in with those spoiled Queen Mary kids?"

"Me? Me?" My voice growing louder with outrage.

"Yes, you. You."

"I'm not the one who turns their nose up at plastic plates." I do my hoity-toity Lynne impression. "Don't you have any silver? This is bad for the environment, oh the inhumanity! Oh, the pollution!"

"My mother died in an oil spill!" Lynne yells, stunning

us both into silence. Then, in a softer voice. "The drilling unit exploded, and she wasn't strong enough to get away."

My entire face burns with shame. I feel as small and disgusting as the maggots in the trash bins. She's right; I did judge her quickly, and then assumed the worst when I found out she wasn't human. Mariss described me as a "spoiled, ungrateful child" to Lynne, and I've done nothing to prove otherwise since she arrived in Fairy Vale.

"I'm sorry."

Lynne scowls and looks away.

I don't want her to think I'm apologizing out of pity. Maybe the back of a speeding garbage truck isn't the best place to have a personal conversation, but I have to make her understand.

"I was jealous of you and Ahkai. I felt like I was losing my best friend. I see that I was wrong now."

She turns to me, and I'm struck by the raw sadness in her face. "Well, you won, not that it was ever a fight. I doubt Auntie will let me out of the sea again."

We survive going around several more roundabouts and cruise down the highway in silence.

"We've reached our destination!" Casper calls from the other side of the truck. It stops at the streetlights by a bright square surrounded by a wharf, and we hop off before the light turns green.

The square is illuminated with blue and yellow lights, our national colors, which leave a glow along the tall Independence Arch.

The towering clock above the parliament building strikes three, reminding me that I should be safe indoors. And I would be, if it wasn't for my own stupidity . . . and Ahkai had to pay the price for it.

The square is empty, with old juice boxes and plastic bags blowing down the steps, across the square and into the wharf. The statue of Barbados's first prime minister, Errol Barrow, points at me like he's scolding me for being out of bed.

The air between me and Lynne is tense and awkward, and we both are clueless about how to act in this new civil partnership.

"Don't go getting any ideas," I tell Lynne, gesturing to the blue glow on the arch as we hurry toward it. "Every time your face lights up, something horrible happens."

This is my way of saying, "I really am sorry."

"Every time you open your mouth, something horrible happens," she pipes up.

That's her way of saying, "You're forgiven."

Lynne and I smirk at each other for a second, and this

time, when her face returns to its regular, glum expression, I can sense the humor behind the frown.

No need for her to smile at all.

Casper bangs on the mural with the pledge of allegiance at the bottom of the arch. "Heartman! Inside!" He waits for a few seconds before knocking again.

"Shhhh!" I glance around the square. "We're going up there." I point up at the symbol.

Of course the coat of arms had to be at the very top of the arch, at least twenty feet high. And there are no stairs.

Casper gives me a boost, and I grab on to the emblem of a pelican to hoist myself up.

"There she goes. The agile leopard climbs the tree for her night's slumber to avert ambushes from larger apex predators."

"Just hush and help me up," Lynne says below me.

I grip the cold, stony edges and start to crawl up the arch, not daring to look down. A scuffling noise to the right attracts my attention. Casper climbs the other end of the arch in an unexpectedly skilled fashion.

I'm one more hoist away from the top of the arch. The dusty coat of arms emblem is to my right, and I can now make out the intricate symbol of a dolphin, a pelican, a tree, and a shield with the motto PRIDE AND INDUSTRY.

My hands ache as I pull myself over the top of the arch. I exhale in relief and rub my muscles, and then check on Lynne.

She is halfway up the column when her polished Mary Jane shoes betray her and she loses her footing.

"Oh no!" I cry.

But Lynne doesn't fall; her left arm is stuck to the column while her body dangles. Lynne flails her arm and legs, unaware that her own body has come to her rescue.

"Helloooo," I call, drawing her attention to her arm. "I thought your skin needed water to become sticky?"

She gapes at her hand with shock. "I don't know how any of this works."

Lynne places her other palm on the stone and then gives it a little tug. There's some resistance, and then it comes away from the rock. She gazes at her hand like she just discovered gold, and then continues to climb the arch.

"Fascinating."

I start, not realizing Casper had reached the top. "The Himalayan tree frog also has an adhesive agent that can adhere to any surface." He uses his hands as a camera to record Lynne's climb.

In no time at all, Lynne joins us atop the monument, which is an unpainted, empty corridor. I'm reaching down to touch the coat of arms plaque, when a soft, threatening voice comes from below.

"Josephine Cadogan, get down here immediately."

I freeze. Mr. Atkins is at the foot of the arch, in a bulletproof vest and military gear, his face full of fury. How did he find us? Did he put a tracking device in my sneakers?

"How dare you risk your neck like this, sneaking out the same night your friend disappears? Have you no regard for your elders?"

I tell him the truth. "Mr. Atkins, Ahkai was kidnapped by the Heartman. Lynne, Casper, and I are going after him."

His face shutters with disbelief and then he narrows his eyes. "Enough of this." He pulls a grappling hook from a pouch around his waist and starts to climb.

"He's going to ruin everything," I shout.

In desperation, I press on the coat of arms, hoping that a door will appear, but nothing happens.

"There's another coat of arms over here!" Lynne says, and bends on the other side to touch it, but then shakes her head.

Mariss is such a liar! I should have known she couldn't

be trusted. Mr. Atkins is already halfway up the arch. Would fate be so cruel to let us get this far, only to be dragged back to Fairy Vale by an irate teacher?

I pull out my flashlight and shine it frantically around the area.

"What's that?" Lynne asks. "Under your feet." I step aside and gaze at what I thought were cracks in the cement. On closer examination, it's a carving of the coat of arms inside the stone. *Step on a crack, break your mother's back.* Why does Mariss have to speak in riddles?

I get to my knees and rub the symbol, but still, nothing happens. I release a scream of frustration.

Casper peers over my shoulder. "So odd that the pelican is standing on its own two feet, when it is usually dancing."

"What are you talking about?" I snap at him. We don't have time for his ramblings. Mr. Atkins will be here at any second.

"Wait," Lynne says, "he's right." She crawls over to the other coat of arms symbol. "This pelican's foot is in the air!"

Casper sits next to me and pushes the pelican's right foot up onto the shield. Right away, the coat of arms carving sinks into the stone, and the arch begins to shake. Lynne, Casper, and I hold on to one another, but thankfully we're already on the floor, unlike Mr. Atkins.

"Earthquake!" he shouts. There's a yell and then the sound of a loud thump when Mr. Atkins hits the ground.

I'm sure he's fine.

The coat of arms starts to spin and then slides across to reveal a dark, gaping hole. I shine the light inside, revealing a narrow staircase . . . and then heavy, dragging footsteps.

I scramble away from the hole. "Someone's coming!"

I'm midway to grabbing the whittling knife when the most wonderful face pops out of the hole.

"Jared!" I rush to hug him, not caring about all the grime and dirt on his body.

"Jo, help me with Coach, please," he says in a weak, tired voice. He attempts to lift a semiconscious Coach Broomes, who has an arm around his shoulder and a face full of cuts and scrapes. Casper and I help them out of the hole.

"Is Coach okay?"

His lips are white and cracked, and his eyes flutter, barely staying open.

"He's dehydrated. He made me drink all his water,"

Jared says in a choked voice. I give him the bottled water from my backpack. As Jared feeds the liquid to Coach, he peers around. "How are we in Independence Square?" He touches the back of his head and winces. "Someone hit me from behind."

"Was it the steel donkey and Heartman? Is Ahkai down there too?"

Jared gapes at me, like I'm the one who got hit in the head. "Did you just say 'Heartman' and 'steel donkey'?"

This is getting us nowhere. Lynne doesn't have a crush on Jared, so she's a lot less polite.

"You can stay here and chat with your boyfriend. I'm going to find Ahkai." She ducks into the hole.

Casper swings his locs over his shoulder. "Well, I'm off to explore the new world!" He follows her inside.

I hurry toward them, but Jared grabs my arm. "Wait, there's nothing down there."

I wish I could explain everything to him, but there's no time. "I'm sorry." I pull my arm away and climb into the darkness.

But then something clutches on to the back of my shirt. "Jared, I have to go." I look back and right into Mr. Atkins's furious eyes. He tightens his grip and starts to lift me from the hole.

"Help!" I scream, struggling to escape.

Someone grabs my hand and yanks me forward with such force that I topple inside, bringing Mr. Atkins into the lair with me.

Then, the stone seal slams shut.

CHAPTER 22

"Noooooo!"

Mr. Atkins's howl echoes in the room, and he bangs on the roof. It sounds like we're in a metal box. Thankfully, I landed on something soft and flat. I exhale and then search my backpack for the flashlight.

"Get off of me," says a muffled voice.

I yelp and scramble to my feet. I shine my light down to see Lynne's scowling face. "Sorry!"

"I'm tired of saving you." She rolls her eyes and re-arranges her dress.

Before I can give a cheeky retort, the light brings rusty, galvanized walls into view, with faded gray lines marked in the steel sheets.

Wait, not marked . . . scratched.

I swerve the light around. We're in a space that looks like a tall chicken coop. And the air is as foul as bird poop too. I cover my nose with my arm. The beam lands on hundreds of scratch marks from the Heartman's countless victims, who must have clawed their fingernails into the walls, trying to escape.

I force myself to remain calm. Jared said there was nothing down here, but surely he didn't mean nothing *nothing*. There must be some way out of this stinky pen.

But there are no doors, or windows, or any kind of exit. All that's left is the desperate markings of people who lost all hope.

Not just people.

Children.

Most of the scratch marks are lower to the ground; only a few of the marks reach my height.

My heart starts to race and I take a deep breath. *Do not panic.*

I spot the light on the ground and roof, hoping to see another sign of the coat of arms carving in the cement but there's none. Maybe someone could open the hatch from above. But who else knows about the pelican's foot, other than Mariss? She would come to rescue Lynne, wouldn't she? But I have my doubts. Mariss isn't known for having a kind heart. My quest to save Ahkai seems to have ended before it began. I am seconds away from joining Mr. Atkins in banging on the roof.

"Are you going to stand there gawking all night or help me find a way out?"

I swing the light toward Lynne's voice and see her feeling around the steel walls, pushing on random spots.

She's right. There has to be some secret exit. Hope blooms in my chest. Thank God I'm not here alone and with someone able to keep a cool head.

"You need light?" I ask, beaming it in the area.

She pauses. "I can see."

I don't ask any more questions. Casper, Lynne, and I run our hands carefully along the rusty steel, feeling for a hidden door or button.

There is a long, long sigh, and then Mr. Atkins abandons his attempt to punch through the cement.

He marches down the stairs. "Troops, we have no choice but to go forward." He takes a penlight from his pouch, and though it's tiny, its beam is much brighter than mine. "We're in the holding space. If I remember correctly, there are three rooms. We have to find the key in each one before getting to the heart of the lair. Then the Heartman has to release us."

"Mr. Atkins." I speak in a careful, slow tone,

enunciating every word. "What do you mean by *if you remember correctly*?"

"I've been here before," he states, as if we're in a restaurant and not in a mythical underground lair.

"But, but . . ." I clench my fists in anger. "You *knew* the Heartman was kidnapping everyone. You could have told the police! Called in some of your army friends, and instead you did nothing but harass Miss Alleyne!"

"Hush," says Mr. Atkins, spotting his light up and down a panel. "I'm trying to concentrate."

I splutter, too angry and appalled for words. Have all the adults in my life been gaslighting me?

"He's a coward," Lynne says in a soft voice. "He would have let them all die."

Mr. Atkins and Lynne glower at each other so forcefully it's clear that they're going to be enemies from this moment on.

Then he jerks his gaze up above her head. "There it is."

He spots his light on a heart-shaped rust spot at the top of the steel wall. And I don't mean "heart-shaped" like the ones you'd see on a Valentine's Day card either, but the hearts you'd find in a hospital room during an organ transplant.

"We need to feed it."

We all stare at him, clueless.

"With blood. That's the only way to open the door."

Of course the door would *actually* be bloodthirsty. Were we to scratch at the walls until our fingers bled? Is that how other people escaped this room? The space becomes even more stifling. Suppose all the dark spots on the walls are bloodstains and not rust?

Lynne must have had the same thoughts. "How was anyone supposed to know they had to feed a spot with blood?" she exclaims.

"They're not," Mr. Atkins replies. "If the Heartman doesn't choose to let you out, you would starve to death in this space."

Lynne and I exchange horrified glances. If we hadn't accidentally pulled Mr. Atkins inside, we would have died.

Mariss gave me this location to the lair to send me to my death.

"We have blood." Mr. Atkins rolls up one of his sleeves and shines the light on his elbow. He has a painful-looking red slash—probably from when he fell off the arch. He presses a handkerchief against the wound. "But we need to reach the spot. It's higher than before."

Casper and I turn to Lynne.

"But he'll see me," she mutters, glancing at Mr. Atkins.

"We don't have a choice," I reply.

"Speak up, maggots!"

Lynne growls under her breath, marches over to him, and snatches the handkerchief away. She places her palms on the rusty wall, curls her fingers, and then starts to crawl up to the heart-shaped blob.

I wait on Mr. Atkins to react, but apart from a slight twitch of his lips, his stern expression remains the same. He trains his light on the heart-shaped spot until Lynne comes into view and presses the bloody handkerchief into it. The rust spot comes alive at the taste of blood and begins to glow. Then the steel wall starts to crack from the top like glass.

Lynne slides down the galvanized steel and rejoins us, looking quite pleased with herself.

Mr. Atkins studies her and taps his chin. "So what are you, a lizard?"

Lynne releases a few words that no regular kid could utter in front of a teacher without instant detention.

"A sea spirit," I correct him.

"A spirit, eh? Any chance you can do more than sweat glue?"

Lynne ignores him, and Mr. Atkins shoots her a look of disdain.

"The Heartman can yank out our hearts with his bare hands. We need strong people on this team."

Lynne doesn't get to answer.

The crack in the wall reaches the ground, and the panel slides open with a loud creak. I prepare myself for some kind of torture chamber with broken chains and blood-splattered walls.

We have to shield our faces from the startling bright light, and when our eyes adjust, the view in front of me makes my heart flip in my chest.

CHAPTER 23

It's the most beautiful place I've ever seen in my life.

A paradise.

Maybe I hit my head when I first fell into the lair, died, and went to heaven.

We're in a lush forest, brimming with flowers of every color imaginable, as if all the blossoms in existence gathered here first before making their way into the world. The blooms thread across towering trees and around smooth, pearl-white rocks. A dozen small waterfalls flow into a small pool in the middle of the forest, with crystal-blue water—the type you want to drink while you swim in it.

Lynne isn't as impressed by the view. "Great," she

says, in a dull voice. "How are we going to find a tiny key in this place?"

The garden is as big as the school hall, with a thousand hiding places for a small key.

Mr. Atkins scans the area, his face uncertain. "The key isn't like one you'd use to open a door. You have to look for something that doesn't belong."

"What the heck does that mean?" I reply. "I don't belong here. Am I a key?"

"Don't be foolish. Keep your eyes peeled for anything that is out of place. It's the key to moving forward."

"Don't you know what *it* is?" Lynne gives him one of her best scowls. It's nice not to be on the receiving end for once. "Unless you don't remember where you left it."

"Everything has changed." Mr. Atkins's face softens in a way that makes me uncomfortable, before hardening again. "Spread out, troops."

He marches toward the darkest area of the garden, where the waterfall flows over moss-covered boulders. Casper quietly films the environment with his hands. Lynne shrugs and pushes her hands into the soil by a bright green tree.

I head to the pool in the center, not only to search the area but also to splash some of the cool water on my face. Despite the numerous waterfalls and shrubbery, the air remains hot and stifling.

The pool shimmers as I get closer, and the water is so clear that I can see sparkling pebbles at the bottom. I'm about to reach into the water when Casper exclaims in disgust behind me.

"All this bush and no wildlife anywhere to observe. What a shame," he says, kicking a stone.

That's when I become aware of the silence. No sound of the stream moving along the rocks. No chirping birds. The serene forest suddenly seems haunting and unnatural.

It's as if the rose-colored glasses fell from my eyes, because when I look into the pool again, I realize that the sparkling pebbles at the bottom of the pool are not pebbles at all.

"Oh my God . . ." I cry, my voice rising on each word.

I barely register the sounds of Lynne and Mr. Atkins hurrying toward me as I stare into the pool, unable to wrench my eyes away.

"What is it? Did you find the—" Lynne's words fall away when she reaches the pool. "Are those—"

A flicker of disgust passes over Mr. Atkins's face. "Buttons," he confirms in his quiet, hard voice.

Thousands of bright buttons.

A shiver goes down my spine as I spot some shaped like stars, hearts, and flowers. Then a few with drawings of teddy bears and smiley faces.

It's a harsh reminder that despite the beauty of the surroundings, we are in the Heartman's domain—a man who made a deal with the devil and lives to torture children. A monster who collects buttons from his victims' clothing as trophies.

And he has Ahkai.

Did Ahkai's pajamas have buttons? In growing panic, my eyes dart to the different buttons inside the pool to see if I recognize any of them.

"We should stick together," Mr. Atkins says. "Safety in numbers."

That makes sense, but it will significantly slow down the search for the key. That's more time for Ahkai to be in the Heartman's clutches. Or more time for the Heartman and steel donkey to show up in this wretched forest and kill us all.

I notice a large rock by some trees to the left. If I climb to the top, I'd have a good view of the entire garden and be better able to notice anything that "doesn't belong." It could save us some time.

"Lemme just take a quick look over here."

"No, wait!" Mr. Atkins says, but I dismiss him with a

wave of a hand and hurry over to the area.

I'm almost to the rock when it starts to rise from the ground. I stagger backward in astonishment, but my feet are stuck. The rock isn't rising—I am sinking! I've marched right into quicksand.

"Help!" I cry. I struggle harder, but it's like wading in superstrength glue. "Lynne! Mr. Atkins! Casper!" The sand seems to enjoy my movements and presses itself closer around my body.

Casper reaches the area first.

"Casper, wait, no!"

But it's too late. He's already sinking. Casper grabs at the air and falls onto his back. Mr. Atkins appears and lays on his belly, grabs Casper's hand, and manages to drag him from the sand before he sinks below the surface.

"You too hard-ears, Josephine," Mr. Atkins scolds. "See what happens when you don't listen?"

"This is not the time!" I'm now waist-deep in the sludge.

Mr. Atkins doesn't move. For a second, I wonder if he'll leave me to die, but then he goes to a nearby tree and tries to break off a branch.

Lynne pops her head out of a bush; she observes

Casper flat on the ground, Mr. Atkins pulling at the tree, me sinking in the sand, and then her mouth twitches.

"Don't you dare laugh," I growl.

"Stop struggling, you're only making it worse."

"Okay, no problem, I'll just sit here and sink."

"Relax, it's not possible to become fully submerged in quicksand," she says, stepping out of the bush. "It's denser than humans, so your body will naturally float."

"Does it look like I'm floating to you?!" I screech. The sand has now covered the area by my belly button. I reach out to the rock, but it's too far. If the Heartman had to appear now, I'd be a sitting duck, ready to be served on a platter.

A flash of doubt comes across Lynne's face. Mr. Atkins returns with the branch, but it's about a foot too short. I wrestle with the sand, trying to reach it, but I can't . . . and my muscles scream in fatigue. Why is fate so determined to drown me? First in the ocean, and now in quicksand.

"Jo, listen to me, move your legs in a circular movement," Lynne says, a tremor of fear in her voice. "That will make the sand more viscous—"

"What does that even mean?!"

"It should be easier to move."

"It's not working!" I'm submerged up to my chest. Mr. Atkins dashes off to the trees, to find a longer branch, I assume.

"Okay, you have to calm down, you're making it worse."

"I am calm!" I scream.

"Listen, I have a confession." Lynne comes as close to the sand as possible. "That day in the cane field? The plan *was* to scare you with the chain, but then I felt bad."

"Well, that didn't stop you, did it?"

"Yes, it did, but when I dropped the chain, it stuck to my foot. I was trying to get it off. That's the rattling and stomping you heard."

A smile forms on my face at the image.

Lynne gives me a sheepish look. "And in the yard with Inkblot too. I wasn't deliberately trying to scare you; I was spying on you and Ahkai, and Inkblot jumped on me and wouldn't get off."

A bubble of laughter escapes from my lips as I remember how Inkblot dangled in the air. "You're really bad at revenge."

"Don't you ever say that out loud again," Lynne threatens, but she's holding back a smile.

What would Ahkai say if he saw me and Lynne working together? He'd probably give us his half smile and nod of approval. The grin falls from my face, and I have to hold back tears.

Lynne grows serious. "And now that you're calm, I don't understand why you're still sinking."

I hadn't realized I stopped moving. I immediately resume fighting with the sand.

Lynne gets on her knees and dips her hand in the sand. "Quicksand doesn't work like this; you should be able to float." She rubs it in between her fingers. "This isn't sand! This is pumice."

I try my best to control my panic. Now it's up to my chest. "Thanks, I'm going to die in quick-pumice, not quicksand. Noted."

"No, you don't get it. This is volcanic rock." Her eyes widen. "Do you see any volcanoes around here?"

"It doesn't belong," Mr. Atkins says, dropping the new branch in his hand. "The key."

She gloats at him, and Mr. Atkins regards Lynne with new respect, as if she now deserves the right to breathe. Then he crosses his arms on his chest like a corpse, jumps into the sand, and descends like he's in an elevator.

Casper gets to his feet. He and Lynne eyeball each other and then cannonball into the quick-pumice. They hold themselves ramrod straight and sink as fast as Mr. Atkins.

"Stop struggling, Josephine," Lynne says. "Let it take you."

"You all are insane!" I shout as they disappear. "You could be wrong, Lynne!"

"Let go!" Lynne shouts, before the sand covers her head.

There's no way I'll willingly go to my death. I push to reach the rock, and then, as if the moment couldn't get any worse, a chilling sound penetrates the air.

Reeeeeekkkkkkkkkkkkkkkkkk.

He's here.

The steel donkey's chains echo in the garden, and the leaves in every single tree start to shake. There's no telling which one the Heartman and steel donkey may leap out from. An avalanche of darkness consumes the light, plunging the garden into shadow and sweeping toward me like an incoming wave.

Reeeeeekkkkkkkkkkkkkkkkkkk.

"Oh God, oh God, oh God." I don't know what's worse—to drown in sand—sorry, pumice—or to be mauled by the steel donkey.

Then fate takes the decision away from me.

Something grabs my leg and pulls me downward.

CHAPTER 24

The iron grip tightens on my leg, and I let out a hurtling scream.

Wait, I can scream?

Before I can process that I'm able to breathe, I'm falling. Again.

Falling isn't too bad actually; it's the landing that hurts. For the second time tonight, the breath gets knocked out of me. I lie on the ground, too winded to open my eyes; I feel like an old sock in a washing machine.

"Why is she so hardheaded?" Lynne's frustrated voice comes from above.

"I told you, she doesn't listen. She's going to get us killed, mark my words."

So much for them being enemies forever . . . one mistake on my part and now they're battle buddies.

I open my eyes to see Lynne and Mr. Atkins over me with identical scowls, but they don't hold my attention; the pumice floats above their heads like a khaki sky. My T-shirt and jeans are completely dry, not even a grain of sand on my skin. The giant rock twists out of it, serving as some kind of ladder to go back through the sludge . . . or for something to enter it.

I jump to my feet, startling Lynne and Mr. Atkins. "The Heartman is coming!"

They hightail it from under the floating pumice without any questions, with me following behind.

We appear to be in another Garden of Evil. My stomach churns as I wonder what trophies we may find under the leaves. Broken toys? Ripped clothing? Pacifiers? I squeeze through a tall, green hedge and prepare for the worst.

The hedges split into two rows, forming a short pathway ahead. So far, there's nothing out of the ordinary. These hedges are the same as the ones in those fancy neighborhoods with the giant gates at the entrance. But I doubt we'll be greeted by a bored security guard at the end of this path; the Heartman could be waiting for us with a sickle and a smile.

If it wasn't for my impulsive nature, Ahkai and I would be safe at home in our beds, gathering energy for a full day of shopping for school supplies. I messed up; I have to do everything in my power to save him.

I follow Lynne and Mr. Atkins through the manicured leaves until we reach the end of the path.

In front of us is a massive lawn in a greenhouse, the shimmering glass almost too bright to look at. It's full of hedges sculpted into life-sized animal shapes; if I raised my hand and jumped as high as I could, I still wouldn't reach a giraffe's knee.

"Okay, it'll definitely be harder to find the key in here," Lynne says, gaping at the lawn.

The topiary forms create a twisted maze that seems to have no end. In the middle of the maze is a large watering hole, surrounded by animal sculptures taking a drink.

I had read about creatures called "douens" in the *African and Caribbean Folklore* book. They're faceless children with backward feet who lure you into the bushes, where you're lost forever. Maybe that is the Heartman's plan—to lure us into the maze, where we'll spend the rest of our lives trying to find our way out.

"Whatever we do, let's stick together this time," Mr. Atkins barks. His gaze burns into my back.

"Wait a minute." I look around. "Where's Casper?"

Mr. Atkins groans.

Then, a chilling noise penetrates the air. The angst and pain in the cry brings giant goose bumps to my skin. Is this where the Heartman tortures children? Mr. Atkins whips out a baton from his waist.

"What is that?!" Lynne moves closer to me as the cry gets even louder.

"I don't know, but I hope Casper is in the other direction." I head in the opposite of the terrible sound.

"Wait," Mr. Atkins says, his voice soft. He lowers his baton. "That *is* Casper."

The words barely leave his lips before I am racing toward the cry, forgetting all about sticking together. I don't want to be responsible for another kidnapping.

The ground is covered with that fake, paperlike grass, but I can still hear Lynne and Mr. Atkins following behind me. I turn a corner by a bush gorilla flexing its muscles and pull the knife out of my backpack, ready to defend Casper against whatever monster is attacking him.

I come to a screeching halt when I see Casper alone, on his knees before a family of bush elephants, with his head bowed. He puts his face in his hands, muffling the heart-wrenching sound.

"Casper? What's wrong?"

You'd think this would be his dream place, with so many animals for commentary. He turns to me, his eyes shimmering like glass. I've only seen them so full of grief once before.

"Your wife," I whisper, "this is her work, isn't it?"

Casper wasn't exaggerating when he said her sculptures were masterpieces. I can almost hear the mama elephant trumpeting and wrangling her baby on the lawn.

The Heartman wrecked so many families. He ripped the hearts out of people's chests in more ways than one. Casper's life fell apart when his wife—his heart—was taken. Miss Mo will never recover if I don't get back Ahkai.

Of course, tears start to flow down my cheeks. Here's proof that Casper has been telling the truth all along, that the Heartman *did* kidnap his wife. This impressive greenhouse represents the years of work she must have completed while trapped here. It's horrible enough to lose someone you love, but it's worse when you have to endure years of people laughing at your pain. What would I have done if no one believed that the Heartman kidnapped Ahkai? If I had to venture into the lair alone? I realize Lynne turned her back on her only family to help me save Ahkai, and I've never even thanked her for it.

I glance at her over my shoulder. To my surprise, there are tears streaming down her cheeks as well; for once she's not trying to hide her emotions. Our eyes meet again—for real this time, all our masks off and our souls bare and vulnerable. My heart swells inside my chest, making more room to let others in. When the emotions become too overwhelming, I break the gaze and turn back to Casper.

"Casper," I draw close to him. "We have to find the key. It could lead us to your wife, to Jennifer."

It's not likely that she's alive, but I choose to hope. I have to believe that we'll all make it out of this lair safely.

Casper caresses the baby elephant, his bottom lip quivering. "I will wait here, in case she comes back."

A determined look comes over his face, and he plants himself onto the ground. I pull on his arm, but he wrenches it away. He swings his head left and right, as if he expects his wife to amble down the row any minute.

We can't leave him here. Not alone. I plead to Lynne and Mr. Atkins with my eyes.

Mr. Atkins, still with his stern expression, strides over

to Casper. I expect him to insist that we don't have time for tantrums, to command him to be "at ease" or whatever he tells his troops. But Mr. Atkins places his gloved hand on Casper's jaw, in a gentle manner that is so contrary to his rough nature.

"Let's go, Sidney, we'll find her together," he says, in his quiet voice.

Casper starts to shake his head, but Mr. Atkins puts his other hand on the opposite cheek, holding his face in place.

"Your love will lead you to each other."

This is not the pep talk I would have expected from Mr. Atkins, but it does the trick. Casper flings his locs over his shoulders, gets to his feet, and surveys the space. No commentary. No camera hands, nothing. He is as serious as a soldier about to go to war.

Mr. Atkins puts an arm around Casper's shoulder, and together we walk through the maze of animal sculptures. Casper examines each animal carefully to find one that doesn't belong. For some reason, the mission feels less hopeless. It's no longer *if* we find the key but when.

I touch Lynne's arm, and we fall a little ways behind Casper and Mr. Atkins. I may not get another private moment to thank her.

Lynne tilts her head, waiting, but somehow it's hard to get the words from my mouth. I wish Miss Alleyne were here, well, not here in the Heartman's domain, but able to whisper the right thing to say in my ear.

Just be nice.

"When we get out of here, after we find Ahkai," I say to Lynne, "we could do some beach cleanups or save sea turtles or whatever. It doesn't matter if you're not allowed on land; we'll come to you."

Lynne jerks her head back in surprise. She doesn't respond at first, but then a smile grows on her face, wider and wider until two dimples appear on her cheeks.

Mr. Atkins glances back at us in confusion, most likely wondering why we're acting like we're strolling through a park and not on a life-or-death mission.

I was not ready for the warmth that filled my insides at Lynne's smile; I'm eager to keep the sunshine on her face a bit longer.

"It would be our new mission—Operation Save the Ocean. You need a code name. What's your last name? Lynne who?"

She shrugs. "Just Lynne."

The most amazing thing happens next—I get the urge to share.

I lean in close to her ear. "What about Edghill? That was my mum's last name, before she married my dad. Your initials would be L.E., and code name Lima Echo. It suits you."

"Yea," Lynne replies, nodding her head slowly. Then she beams. "It does, doesn't it?"

I move away, finally satisfied. I may not have said the words "thank you," but now Lynne understands she's part of our team. She belongs with me and Ahkai now.

Up ahead, Mr. Atkins has gone still, his eyes on me and wide with shock.

"What?" I ask, dread unfurling in my belly.

Then I hear it—humming so strong the bushes around us start to tremble.

I look up, and oh my gosh, black dots emerge from the sculptures, some clusters so thick they block the roof of the greenhouse.

Giant. Black. Bees.

The Heartman sent thousands of insects after us. Talk about overkill—a hundred bees could have easily done the job.

I have no idea how to fight them. There's no bug spray in my backpack. Even if there were, it would only be enough to kill a few of them.

A swarm of bees drop like bombs from a plane, aimed right at our heads.

"Smoke!" Casper exclaims. "Bees stay away from smoke."

Mr. Atkins yanks a tusk from a nearby rhinoceros, pulls a lighter from his pouch and sets it aflame. Then he sets fire to the rest of the sculpture. The flames catch and spread to the other dry animal sculptures like they've been doused in gasoline. Black smoke billows into the air.

We race away from the area, shielding our faces from the heat. The bees fly after us, the fire not slowing down their attack. Mr. Atkins waves the burning branch above our heads, and the insects swerve away. But it won't be long until they dive at our heads again.

The bees are as big as cricket balls, with orange and black stripes. They have huge black teardrop eyes and pincers like a lobster. I do *not* want to feel those stings in my flesh.

"These don't look like normal bees to me!" I yell as we race through the maze. Whatever "normal" means in the Heartman's domain.

"Not bees," Casper shouts, "murder hornets!"

"Who cares!" I yelp.

"A honeybee dies after a single use of its stinger,"

Casper replies while panting. "Murder hornets can sting over and over. They're known for decapitating their prey; it's fascinating, really. I heard their sting feels like a hot nail being plunged into your skin."

This new information encourages an extra burst of speed from everyone.

"It injects a venom that can shut down the nervous system—"

"Enough, Casper!" we yell.

Some of the murder hornets dive again, but the tusk torch is almost gone. Mr. Atkins throws what's left at them.

That was our last means of defense. There's nothing to protect us from their next attack.

"Inside the moose!" Mr. Atkins yells, which is a phrase that would have made me giggle at any other time. We break right, diving into the moose sculpture and climbing up into its belly. But the branches are frail and not designed to hold any weight at all. The murder hornets hover around the moose, as if they know it won't hold us for long.

"There." I point at the watering hole, which is now a few meters away. "They can't follow us into the water."

Mr. Atkins nods. "We need a distraction."

"Some species of wasps—"

Casper doesn't get to finish the sentence. We get a distraction that we didn't bargain for.

The branches crack under Casper, and, with a surprised yell, he falls out of the moose belly.

CHAPTER 25

"Casper!" I cry in horror.

The murder hornets don't let him hit the ground. They swoop down and cover his entire body, and a Casper-shaped cluster of insects rises into the air. The rest of the swarm parts to make room for them. We can't hear him screaming, but the cluster mimics the movement of his flailing arms and legs.

Mr. Atkins shouts, "Move, now *now!*"

Lynne grabs my hand and jumps, pulling me out of the moose.

We hit the ground running. I look over my shoulder, trying to see what the hornets have done with Casper, but the packed swarm blocks everything from view.

The murder hornets don't like giving chase. Their

hum grows more frantic behind us as we race through a herd of bush zebras. They're close, so close I can feel their vibrations inside my ears. At any moment I expect to be yanked into the air to join Casper.

But somehow we make it to the watering hole. We run into the pond and dive into the safety of the water.

I expected the water to be shallow, so I'm caught off guard when it's so deep I'm unable to see the bottom of the pond. The water is murky blue but still clear enough for me to watch Mr. Atkins shrug out of his bulletproof vest. I follow his lead and pull off my backpack as well.

It floats upward, and as soon as it gets to the surface, a swarm of murder hornets attack the bag with their clawed legs. A few of the murder hornets dare to crawl under the straps, jamming stingers that must be at least two inches long into the fabric, before popping out of the water.

That could have been my head. Their stingers would have ripped it to shreds.

Then I realize it was a huge mistake to jump into the pond. These aren't normal insects, which would fly off to search for food somewhere else. Just like when we were in the moose's belly, the hornets are patient enough to wait until we run out of breath.

"I can breathe!" Lynne exclaims.

I jolt, releasing a few bubbles of precious air. I'm still not accustomed to hearing voices underwater.

But this is good news. Lynne can stay in the water for as long as needed; one of us may get out of this situation alive. I give her an encouraging nod and then concentrate on staying calm. Nothing burns air faster than panic, and I can hold my breath for only about a minute.

If I don't make it out of this situation, and it doesn't seem like I will, Lynne has the best chance of saving Ahkai. For a moment, I picture Daddy and Miss Alleyne crying at my funeral, with Ahkai giving the eulogy. I bet he'd simply say "Josephine was awesome," and walk off the stage. Despite the life-threatening situation, amusement rises up inside me. I wish I could be there to see it. There would be lots of tears—continuous bawling from Miss Mo for sure, but at least Ahkai won't be alone; he and Lynne would have each other.

My eyes start to burn. If I wasn't underwater, I would be able to feel the tears on my cheeks. We could have all had so much fun together, had I not been so afraid to lose Ahkai. We will never get a chance to do operations together. I've never had a friend who is a girl before. Maybe Lynne and I would have had sleepovers, and I could talk to her about my crush on Jared. I mourn for all the moments that could have been had I been more welcoming.

The burning sensation in my chest grows stronger, and my stomach contracts. How long has it been? Forty seconds? I don't have much longer, and those murder hornets aren't going anywhere.

Mr. Atkins hugs his body, his eyes closed. He's not moving at all, not even to kick his feet. Yet he doesn't sink. His face is completely relaxed, no pinched lips or anything; the only movement comes from his mustache, curling in the water.

Is he dead?

The thought raises my heart rate even higher and makes me lose a few more bubbles of air.

"Jo, please, tell me what to do." Lynne grabs my shoulders. "I want to help, but I don't know what to do."

I want to reassure her, but I can't while resisting the urge to take a deep, watery breath. The murder hornets get more animated above the surface, as if they know they don't have to wait much longer for their prey.

Lynne brings her mouth to mine and blows air into it. I stiffen, then release my breath into hers and try to inhale as much as possible. Some of the pressure eases but not for long. The burn in my chest returns moments later—maybe sea spirits don't have a lot of oxygen.

I shake my head. It didn't work.

"Tell me what to do," she begs again, her eyes wide with panic. "Now is the time I want you to be bossy!"

I try to mime "Save Ahkai" by tracing his name in the water and pumping my fists.

"What?! What?! I don't understand."

This is pointless. Instead of trying to do charades, I spend my last conscious moments giving her some comfort. I press my hands over my heart and then put them on her cheeks, hoping that she understands the final message—"It's okay."

"This isn't how this ends," she snarls, her tiny features twist in anger.

Lynne tries to share air with me again, but the burning returns even faster, and I gag as a little bit of salt water rushes down my throat.

Then Lynne's freckles start to glow, and her spine shifts from side to side. The heat from her body turns the water warm. She's trying to call for help again, but there are no fish in this pond to come to our rescue. She thrusts her hands above her head and makes swirling circles with her fingers.

"Auntie M moves her hands like this." She closes her eyes, and her blue freckles glow even brighter. A few murder hornets drop into the water, attracted by the light. They struggle in the water and then go still, but most of the swarm waits above the surface, so frenzied that they hit into one another.

Then the water shifts. My eyes widen as the surface shivers and the water splashes at the top. Some of the swarm scatters. *She's doing it!* I'm getting lightheaded now; I won't last much longer.

But then the water stills as quickly as it began. Lynne's hands start to shake, and she balls them into fists.

"I can't do it, I'm not strong enough," Lynne sobs.

Another voice flows through the water. A light musical lilt that could be an angel's song. "I got this."

I open my eyes to see Mr. Atkins, alert and smiling . . . *and speaking underwater.* Am I hallucinating? Maybe my brain is malfunctioning from lack of oxygen.

Mr. Atkins's feet melt together, and his army-green jacket turns into glittering green and blue scales. His bottom half extends and twists into a gold-and-black snake's bottom. His eyes turn bright yellow, and his face starts to shrivel, beginning with his black Colonel Sanders mustache, burning away like a piece of paper.

Then his head explodes into flame. Wait, not fire, but

a curly blond afro, and Mr. Atkins's face melts into a familiar, smug expression.

It can't be . . . but it is.

My eyes trace the gold spiral pendant against her chest.

Mariss.

CHAPTER 26

I am so stunned I inhale salt water.

Mariss twirls her hands, and the salt water changes direction in my throat, gushing back out through my nostrils and mouth. I make the same noise as Daddy when he's gargling mouthwash.

Mariss throws her hands in the air, blasting the pond water from the hole. A ball of water swirls under my feet, and pushes me to the top of the hole. I land on top of a bush zebra and tumble to the ground.

My backpack drops onto my face with a loud smack. I shove it away and clutch my throat, coughing, and also trying not to since it hurts so much.

The murder hornets are trapped in water bubbles

at the top of the greenhouse. They are furious; they struggle in the water balls, making them shake like Jell-O. Mariss sits like a queen on top of a bush giraffe's head, with her arms outstretched, and her snake bottom wrapped around the giraffe's neck, legs, and then continuing into the gaping hole that had once contained the pond.

Mr. Atkins is Mariss . . . or is Mariss Mr. Atkins? I can't be sure. But if it wasn't for both of them, I would be dead.

A sopping-wet Lynne marches over to Mariss. She puts her hands on her hips, something I'd never dare to do before any grown-up, especially one who can kill you with fangs. "Why didn't you tell me that we can change into other humans?" she demands.

Mariss simply stares down at Lynne without answering. Lynne loses a bit of confidence, and her hands fall to her sides.

"We would have gotten to that lesson had you not abandoned your classes," Mariss finally replies.

"How much more sewing, Latin, and singing did I have to do before we got to *human metamorphosis*?"

I clear my throat, eager to ask my burning question before Lynne gets more hysterical. "Have you always been Mr. Atkins?"

Now Mr. Atkins's animosity to Miss Alleyne and Daddy makes sense. And also, his fear of the silk cotton tree. But how long has Mariss been posing as my grumpy primary school teacher? Two years prior, was it Mariss who locked me out of the classroom when I was only a minute late? *She would be that petty.*

Mariss sucks her teeth. "This may come as a shock, but not everything is about you, Josephine. I've only been impersonating him a few weeks. He's back in the cave, locked in the guest room."

The words trigger a memory of gruff cries and loud banging when we were escaping Mariss's cave. I was too busy fleeing for my life for them to register. "Oh my God, that was Mr. Atkins?"

Mariss rolls her eyes. "He's fine, relax. The lionfish actually like him, but we don't have time for this." She gestures toward the trapped murder hornets with her chin.

"But why? Why Mr. Atkins? You can be anyone, so why him?"

All this time I was assuring myself Mariss was gone from my life, and she was only wearing different skin. I've never trusted Mariss, but I didn't understand the depths of her deviousness. I grow wary, wondering what lengths she would go to teach Lynne a lesson.

"We don't have time for this," Mariss snaps. "Go and find the key so we can get out of this place."

"You said you've been here before," Lynne says slowly, and the two of us draw the same conclusion at the same time. "Are you working with the Heartman, Auntie M?"

I reach for my backpack and then remember I used up my snake repellent in her cave. Although, any attack on her now would release the murder hornets from their watery cages.

A look of hurt flashes in Mariss's eyes. "You really think I would put you through all of this?"

"I didn't think you cared," Lynne replies, but her voice is different. Softer, filled with a bit of hope.

Tell her you care! I want to scream the words at Mariss. Doesn't she understand that Lynne has spent her life moving from place to place, with nowhere to call home? I'm so grateful for my daddy, who may not be able to afford a phone or laptop for me but always makes sure I feel loved and protected.

"Don't get all emotional on me now. A few weeks living with humans and you're getting soft."

As soon as the words left her mouth, Mariss regretted them. Lynne's shoulders drop, and she turns away, missing the look of remorse on Mariss's face. If she could, I bet Mariss would swap her water-control powers for Miss Alleyne's way with words.

Lynne folds her arms, her body still turned away from Mariss. "I guess I'm just weak, like my mother."

Mariss regains her cold expression. "And I'm just a monster."

That's when I finally see the family resemblance. They're both as stubborn as a popcorn kernel stuck in a tooth. They're both hurting and in desperate need of affection, but have no idea how to ask for it. So instead, they berate each other and themselves. Someone has to help them, and since there's no licensed therapist around, I guess the job is mine.

I point my finger at Mariss, as if she's a witness on trial.

"You did all of this, took Mr. Atkins's place, *because* you were worried about Lynne. You wanted to keep an eye on her. But, I could be wrong, and you don't care—"

"Of course I care!" Mariss cracks under my cross-examination. "She is my family!"

The silence is deafening, and then another brilliant smile spreads across Lynne's face as she turns to Mariss.

"I heard you; you don't have to shout, Auntie M," she says, her eyes twinkling.

Even Mariss can't maintain her cold facade under Lynne's happy face. "Your mother was weak, but not all the time," she says softly. "She spent her entire life being obedient and not daring to come out of the ocean." Mariss's eyes flicker with pain. "And the one time she was supposed to be a coward, she tried to be brave and got herself killed."

"I—I don't understand," says Lynne.

"Your mother went back for a human, tried to save them from the explosion." All the emotion drains from Mariss, leaving her looking tired and defeated.

Mrs. Edgecombe had said last year that sea spirits help their followers with emotional suffering, but what happens if the spirit is the one overwhelmed with grief? I never thought I could feel sorry for Mariss, but it must be terrible to have healing powers but be unable to use them on yourself.

A range of emotions pass across Lynne's face: shock, awe, sadness, and then finally settles on pride. She reaches a hand out to Mariss, as if she wants to comfort her, but then changes her mind.

"I told you, I can take care of myself," Lynne reassures her.

"She can, you know," I add. "Lynne is smart, and cool,

and if you can't see that, then too bad for you."

Lynne shoots me a grateful look, and Mariss's face immediately twists in anger.

"I *told* you not to follow this idiot down here. She would have been out of my hair for good. If we're not out of this lair by sunrise—the end of the full moon cycle—then we'll be stuck here forever."

"WHAT?!" both Lynne and I shout.

"That's in—" I check my watch. "Thirty-three minutes!" Then I remember how easily she gave the directions to the lair. "You wanted me to be trapped down here."

Mariss shrugs. "That was the plan, but I didn't account for the world's most stubborn niece. I don't know where you get that from."

I shake my head. "You're always going to try to control people, aren't you? Then blame us when we do whatever we can to get rid of you."

I expect Mariss to bare her fangs at me or maybe hit me in a face with a murder hornet bubble, but instead, she does the most unexpected thing.

"What do you know?" she says, cocking her head at me. "A broken clock is right twice a day." Then she turns to Lynne and sighs. "I know you can take care of yourself. That useless knowledge about soil came in handy today. I was . . . proud."

Lynne's mouth falls open in shock.

"I'll try to be more open-minded, and we'll figure out your transformation together. I expected you to return to the ocean when your freckles glowed, but you didn't. That's actually when I, um, borrowed Mr. Atkins."

"What about me?" I ask. "Don't I get an apology? After all, you tried to kill me, *again*."

Mariss scoffs. "Nah, I'm good." She pauses. "But in the spirit of our new . . . alliance, there is something else you should know. If you want Ahkai back, the Heartman requires a sacrifice."

I groan. "Why didn't you tell me? What kind of sacrifice? I didn't bring anything . . ." My voice trails away when I see the look on Mariss's face. It's filled with sympathy. She's never looked at me with such pity, and that's when I understand the type of sacrifice the Heartman will demand.

"It's me, isn't it? I'm the sacrifice."

"No," Lynne gasps.

Mariss doesn't deny it. "Yes, he will want a heart. And don't even think about offering yours," Mariss snaps at Lynne.

Lynne tenses as she waits for my reaction, as if she's expecting me to abandon the plan to save Ahkai. I would never leave my best friend to die. It was my fault he was outside after dark, my ignorance that got him kidnapped in the first place. There was a big chance I wouldn't make it out of the lair, but now that my death is all but certain, I wish I had ignored Bernard and hugged Daddy a little bit longer.

I square my shoulders and lift my head. "So be it."

Then the murder hornet bubbles start to shake more forcefully, and Mariss scowls up at them. "I can't hold them all day—and we have thirty-two minutes now until sunrise. Check the maze for the key."

Lynne rushes toward the maze, but I stop her.

"The maze is just a distraction. We've already found the key." I wipe a drop of water from my face and put it in my mouth. "Salt doesn't belong in a watering hole."

Mariss and Lynne look totally gobsmacked that two sea spirits missed that fact. Unfortunately, I don't have time to gloat.

Lynne and I peep into the gaping hole, which must be at least twenty feet deep and bordered with brown jagged rock.

"There!" At the far end of the watering hole is a small, square opening. "Can you make another one of those water escalators?" I ask Mariss, not wanting to risk the climb down the rocks.

She shakes her head. "I move my hands now and all this water comes crashing down on us. Along with the bees."

"Murder hornets," Lynne and I correct her together.

"You can do it, Lynne," Mariss urges.

Lynne shakes her head wildly. "No, no I can't."

"Yes, you can," I encourage her. "Remember what Ahkai says, *just trust yourself.*" Then I put my hands on her cheeks. I guess that's our thing now.

"Close your eyes and take a deep breath." Mariss's voice is soothing, but now I can hear the strain underneath it. I glance at her; her shoulders are tense, and a bead of sweat rolls down her forehead. But to her credit, she doesn't get impatient or snappy.

Lynne follows the instructions, raising her hands in the air.

"You have to concentrate on the flow of the water and become one with it; imagine it flowing through your body. Move from side to side if that helps."

A few seconds later, Lynne's cheeks start to glow, and her waist shifts like a bouncy spring. A puddle of water at our feet starts to shake.

"That's it, that's it. Good girl."

The puddle of water rises in the air, up to my knees. Lynne opens her eyes and beams at the dingy puddle like it's a newborn baby. "I'm doing it! I'm doing it!" The puddle shakes and starts to fall apart.

"Concentrate," Mariss says in a gentle but warning tone.

"Sorry." Lynne breathes again, and the puddle stabilizes.

"Okay now, Josephine, get on."

I open my mouth to say "Hell naw," but then I stop. I told Lynne to trust her powers, so I have to show that I trust them too. I say a prayer in my head and step on the water ball. It's wobbly at first, but I find my balance.

"Maintain the flow. Remember, you and the water are one. You don't command it; you are part of it."

Lynne steps onto the bubble and I have no choice but to join in her dance; it's either that or be shoved off by her hips. I hold my breath as we float into the hole, swaying to Lynne's magical beat. I don't dare to breathe, not until the water touches the rock at the bottom of the hole.

"I knew you could do it!" I throw my hands around Lynne, and we hug and squeal.

"Girls . . ." Mariss warns from above.

It's time to go.

Then, everything around us moves before we can get the chance. The walls shake, and the jagged rocks rumble and start to close in.

"Run!"

Lynne doesn't have to tell me twice. We sprint toward the square door.

Bam! I look back to see chunks of the rock slam together, like they're trying to take a bite out of us. Mariss screams Lynne's name in the distance, then there's a large splash and loud buzzing.

I don't bother to turn around again. I focus on the square ahead, pumping my arms and pushing my head forward like I would when racing down the cricket pitch, desperate to make it back to the base before the wicketkeeper breaks the stumps. Behind us the rocks bang together, and pebbles hit into the back of my neck.

I dive when I get close enough to the square, making sure to tuck my elbows into a ball.

Made it! I roll into a small room, similar to the first chicken coop space, except it's made out of wood.

I turn to Lynne, but she's not beside me.

I whirl around to see her still running toward the square, her face red and hair wild.

"Hurry up!" I scream. She's almost here. Lynne reaches her hand out to me.

Bam!

The rocks slam together, crushing Lynne and leaving only a tiny crack in the stone.

CHAPTER 27

A cold, numbing sensation comes over me as I stare at the rocks.

I tilt my head. Is it possible I'm dreaming and none of this—the Heartman, the steel donkey, the lair—is real?

I squeeze my eyes shut. "Please please please please." I push a trembling finger forward and pray feverishly to feel nothing but blank space ahead. I'll open my eyes and see the old brass clock in my bedroom, and then I'll rush next door to tell Ahkai about this wild nightmare.

When my finger touches the hard, damp rock, a sob escapes my mouth. And then another. And then I can't stop them from tumbling out.

I've never seen anyone die before. My heart aches, like someone is squeezing the life out of it inside my chest. I can't imagine how Daddy felt when he woke up next to Mum and realized she wasn't breathing. Now I understand why he never left his room and wanted to stop living, even though I still needed him. Daddy's love for me got him through the pain.

Those thoughts bring me to my feet. I have to find Ahkai; Lynne would count on me to rescue him. I have thirty minutes to do it. I take a few short breaths to calm my mind. *You can do this.* I turn around and almost collapse on seeing the cloaked figure behind me.

The Heartman stands on a tall pillar; his long black cloak shrouds his entire body and pools around his feet. The dim light above his head finally reveals the face under the wide hat—actually, it's more skull than face. Bone-white and hard, with round flaring nostrils and stark-white eyeballs without pupils. His cracked lips are as white as his face but with black lines running through them like tiny polluted rivers.

The Heartman stares down at me with his empty gaze. My heart beats so hard I'm sure he can hear it. My brain urges me to run, to fight, to do anything other than wait for him to reach down and rip my heart from my chest. Though I don't know why he wants it—it's bruised and broken right now.

No, not broken . . . not yet.

A sudden wave of anger bursts through my fear. The Heartman ruined Casper's life when he took his wife and then suffocated him with murder hornets. Lynne hadn't even started to live before he crushed her, leaving nothing of her to mourn. He's stolen more than enough hearts since I entered his lair. He's had more than enough sacrifices, yet will still demand my heart in exchange for Ahkai's.

It's not fair.

I may not have the power to change his rules, but I can face him without cowering. He doesn't have to see my fear.

I steel myself against his gaze. "I made it through your rooms; now I want you to let Ahkai go."

He doesn't respond.

I move to the side, out of his line of sight. The Heartman doesn't budge. Then I take a closer look at the pillar underneath him and read HEARTMAN I chiseled into the stone.

It's a statue.

A very lifelike wax statue.

I exhale and slump over with relief. Mariss had said there were three rooms, and I've only been through two of them—the Garden of Evil and Murder Maze.

Mariss. Did she escape? I glance back at the rocks

again . . . and if she did, does she know about Lynne? I hope I am not the person who has to break the news. *Later.* I'll worry about that in less than thirty minutes.

I exhale and creep around the statue, my heart still thumping. Behind the statue is a white wooden door with a silver doorknob, so normal it seems out of place. It could be the entrance to any Fairy Vale Academy classroom.

I wish so much that I was safe at school right now. Any school. It feels like weeks, not days, since I thought my life was over because I passed to Queen Mary. Now I would give anything for a chance to go to the secondary school.

I don't have time to feel sad. Less than twenty-nine minutes now to get out of here. I push the feelings down as far as I can and walk toward the door.

I turn the knob slowly, and it swings open with a loud creak.

I have to bite my tongue to hold back my scream. So much for hiding my fear. If I thought the first Heartman statue was scary, it's nothing compared to the other wax statues in the room.

At least a dozen statues depict the Heartman in various forms; one with his cloak open to reveal a gaping hole in his bony chest and a bloody heart clutched in his hands. In another, he sits inside a hearse that has coffins jutting out from every window. I tremble at the portrayals, each one more terrifying than the next: the Heartman gorging on hearts, covered in centipedes, crouching in cane fields, and finally the tall, cloaked figure atop the steel donkey. Each statue is so detailed, so realistic, it's impossible to know what is alive or wax.

I'm frozen by the door, my heart beating so loud in my ears I can't hear myself think. I take a deep breath and press my hand against my chest. It helps calm me down, so why is my heartbeat still so loud?

It's at that moment I realize the heartbeats aren't mine. They're coming from the wax figures! As loud as someone banging a fist from the inside of the sculptures. Only my determination to save Ahkai stops me from bolting from the room.

There's no way to tell if the real Heartman is here. He could be right beside me. Everything sounds alive, even as each statue remains fixed on the spot.

But at the end of the room is a sculpture that's not like the others. It's a small replica of the Independence Arch, except there's a waterfall of hot wax flowing from top to bottom. It's clearly the key; the thing doesn't belong.

I move toward the waterfall, but then stop after taking a few steps.

If Lynne were here, she'd scoff and chide me for believing it would be so simple. That I could just walk across this room with no obstacle. This is the last room before I reach the heart of the lair. The last one before I get to Ahkai.

The swell of emotion makes me take another eager step forward, but then I force myself to wait. I can hear Mr. Atkins—well, Mariss—calling me a fool for being so easily tricked.

I crouch behind a statue of the Heartman holding a screaming kid by their feet. The heartbeat gets louder as I get closer to it, but I try to ignore the sound. I reach inside my backpack for my cricket ball and gently roll it toward the circle with the hot wax. None of the statues move as it rolls past them, one by one. *No hidden traps.* I hold my breath, feeling a glimmer of hope. The ball is almost to the wax.

Wham!

The steel donkey jumps into the circle from above and grabs the ball in its teeth. I cover my mouth to hold in my scream and duck lower behind the statue. The steel donkey shakes its head wildly from side to side, the steam from its nostrils fogging up the room and filling it with the stink of damp fur and manure. By the time it's finished, my cricket ball is in pieces.

Just like I would be, had I not listened to my gut.

The steel donkey pushes the ball pieces to a side, one by one, and then prowls along the circle, its chains dragging along the tiles.

There's no way I can make it across the room without it noticing me. The gaps between the figures near the wax waterfall are too wide.

I'm going to have to face the steel donkey, but I have one last defense.

I take Miss Mo's crystal from my pocket, unable to stop my fingers from trembling. It protected me once before; I pray its magic works again. My legs feel like jelly as I step from behind the statue, the crystal outstretched in my hand.

The steel donkey growls, and its eyes burn brighter. It drags one of its feet on the tiles, getting ready to charge.

"Oh please, oh please, oh please." Tears leak from my eyes, and I shake the crystal, hoping to activate it. But the crystal doesn't glow like it did by the silk cotton tree. Instead, it takes on the bright red glow from the steel donkey's eyes.

That's when I understand. It wasn't the crystal that protected me—it was the moon, reflected on the crystal. Mrs. Edgecombe had said that a manifestation of the steel donkey hated the moon's reflection . . . and there's no moon underground. I might as well have stepped out to face the creature holding an earring.

The steel donkey charges, and I leap out of the way at the very last minute, hurtling into a pillar. I get to my feet and race to the waterfall, but it cuts me off and I have to fling myself to the right to avoid its hooves. In desperation, I throw the crystal at its head.

It catches the stone in its mouth, huffs twice, but then swallows it, giving me enough time to retrieve the whittling knife from my backpack. I stab at the steel donkey when it charges again, but the creature releases a ball of steam that burns my eyes. I just manage to roll out of the way of its charge. There's only so long I can play this dangerous dodgeball game until I run out of luck.

Knife in the ground! Mrs. Edgecombe had said a knife in the ground may stop it from attacking. I jam the knife into the floor, hoping that the tip will penetrate the tile.

The blade breaks.

Ahhhhhhh!

I scramble out of the way, and my foot slips. It's a lucky fall, because the steel donkey sails over my head and crashes into a pillar, the steel armor hitting the stone with a loud clang. But that doesn't delay it for long. Almost immediately, the creature gets to its feet and charges again.

What else did Mrs. Edgecombe say?!

Count! The steel donkey can't resist the urge to count. But I used up all the salt at the silk cotton tree; there's nothing else. With no other options, I shake all the contents of the backpack onto the floor; the flashlight, change of clothes, a crumpled five-dollar bill . . . and a bunch of black-eyed peas.

I had forgotten about those! I say a silent thank-you to Miss Mo. The peas bounce over the tiles, rolling in every direction.

The steel donkey rears its legs and then tries to trap the black-eyed peas in its hooves. I don't wait around for it to count them.

I seize the moment to race toward the waterfall and jump into the hot wax.

CHAPTER 28

Though I'm sure the hot wax waterfall is the key, I still brace myself for the burn.

Instead, the wax flows over my body like a cool lotion. It's so refreshing that I pause to enjoy the moment; all the sweat and grime on my skin drips away with the wax.

I open my eyes to the world's most extravagant game room. A road tennis court, basketball court, a running track, and too many pool tables to count. On my left are shelves full of every board game imaginable, the boxes pristine and untouched. An arcade with a wide range of vintage machines and PlayStation and Nintendo consoles. There's even a small Ferris wheel in the middle of the room behind a few bumper cars. The flashing fluorescent lights are so bright they hurt my eyes.

"Josephine, you're here!"

I turn to my right to see Casper and feel a rush of relief.

Casper lounges on a lawn with a litter of lion cubs. A few of them paw at his swinging locs. There are more bush animals on the lawn, but in addition to the usual lions, elephants, and giraffes are sculptures of people. Wait, not people, the same man in different poses. He is broad-shouldered with short locs; the artist has paid careful attention to his face, shaping his eyes, a pointed nose, and smiling full lips with the leaves and branches.

It's only when Casper lifts a cub from his hair and grins at me that I recognize the face. Dozens of depictions of Casper, no, of Sidney. It's hard for me to come to terms with the two versions, especially since Casper's face and arms are now swollen and lumpy from murder hornet stings.

"Meet my wife!" Casper pulls a small woman with locs almost as long as his from behind a deer. She smiles shyly and waves garden shears at me. I raise my palm, still in shock.

"You and Ahkai must join us for dinner tomorrow," Casper says, still beaming at his wife. "If he's finished studying by then."

Casper points at a tiny space between the arcade and

the lawn. It's easy to miss among all the flashing pinball machines. Ahkai, still in his faded T-shirt and pajamas, sits at a table before a mountain of books. He takes one book from the stack, and four more magically appears to replace it.

"Ahkai!"

He's alive! I run across the lawn, jumping over a lion cub, who then races behind me. Ahkai hasn't looked up from the book, and as I get near to him I bang into an invisible barrier, like a bird into a window. I wince and then push against the barrier; it's a transparent, plastic bubble.

"Ahkai! Can you hear me?" I shout, scratching at the plastic. He seems unhurt, with no scratches or cuts, but he doesn't look my way. Maybe the bubble is sound-proof and made from some kind of one-way material, where I can see him, but he can't see me.

I instinctively reach for the knife from my backpack before remembering I left everything in that awful wax museum. Ahkai turns the page, gazes longingly at the tall book stack, and then starts to speed-read, flipping the pages faster.

A large ginger tabby jumps onto the desk. *Is that Simba?!* It can't be, but it is. Ahkai's old cat nudges Ahkai's hand to get attention.

"He can't hear you. He's busy with his heart's desires."

I whirl around, searching for the source of the high-pitched, gleeful voice. "Who said that?"

"I did."

A black bumper car turns, a small boy in a gold velvet robe and sunglasses palming the steering wheel with one hand. He sips on some brown liquid in a crystal glass. "Forgive my manners, would you like some aged gooseberry juice? I made it myself."

Another one of the Heartman's victims, probably kidnapped from another town.

"Little boy, we have to get out of here." I check my watch. Sunrise is in eighteen minutes. I have to find a way to get Ahkai out of that bubble. My eyes are drawn to Casper's wife and the sharp shears in her hand—those should do the trick.

The boy giggles, regaining my attention. He's missing two teeth in the top row; he couldn't be more than nine years old.

"Why would I leave, when everything I want is right here?" He takes another sip of his drink.

I start to get flustered. "Listen, we have to go before the Heartman shows up. Do you know a way out of here?"

Then the steel donkey bursts through the wax, his steel armor clanging.

"Get out of the way!" I yell as it charges toward us. But I'm the only one who reacts. Casper and his wife continue to chat on the lawn, as if a stray dog hurtled past them and not a deadly mythological creature. Ahkai still hasn't lifted his head from his book.

To my surprise, the steel donkey completely ignores me and heads straight to the boy, who leaps out of the bumper car with outstretched arms. But instead of gutting him, the steel donkey licks his face with a giant red tongue, knocking the glass of juice from his hands.

"Ernest, enough!" the boy exclaims, and the steel donkey sits by his feet. It gazes at me with its fiery eyes and a gust of steam leaves its nostrils.

"Calm down, Ernest," the boy says, scratching its ears. "She is our guest now. She found the keys and passed all my tests. Welcome to my lair, Josephine."

"But—but." I survey the boy from head to toe.

He pokes his tongue between the missing space in his teeth. "I'm still growing."

The boy doesn't reach past my hips. There's no way he could be the foreboding cloaked creature that's been stalking us all this time.

"Oh, I can explain," he says with a cheeky grin. He bounces over to an area full of carnival headpieces and feathered masks, and pulls out a pair of stilts. He slips them on and then drapes a long black cloak around his shoulders.

Now he's at least ten feet tall. He smirks at me from above, his face practically hidden in the cloak's collar. No wonder I didn't see his face back at the silk cotton tree, when Casper knocked the hat off his head. I recall how the shadow bent in half when the steel donkey got spooked by the moonlight.

"Why—why would you put us through all of this?" I ask, my voice rising.

The Heartboy shrugs. "I'm bored."

I blink several times, absolutely flabbergasted. "You nearly killed me, you *killed* Lynne, out of boredom!" I start looking for a weapon; I don't need a circle of sea salt to know he's evil.

He shrugs again. "What would you prefer? That I rip your heart out your chest like my father would, and all the Heartmen before him? News flash: collecting organs is boring. And do you realize when you kill people, you have no one left to talk to?"

He gestures around the empty game room and points at Casper's wife. "Good thing I begged my father to let Jennifer live, else I would have been stuck here alone when he died. My ancestors repaid our debt a long time ago, so it's time to change tradition."

"I don't understand what you mean."

A dark, cunning look comes over his face, an expression that seems too devious for a nine-year-old to display. He may look like a kid, but who knows how many years he's actually been alive.

"I'm still interested in hearts, Josephine. How they race, what makes the blood rush through them, what makes them . . . stop. I'm especially interested in hearts' desires right now—they inspire me to create more fantasy rooms for my entertainment."

His gaze bores into mine, as if he's taking a glimpse into my soul. His eyes get brighter, and he licks his lips like he's seen some mouthwatering dessert in a store window. I feel that familiar urge to go closer to him and glance away.

I need to make the deal before he distracts me. I check my watch again. Thirteen minutes until sunrise.

"I found all your keys. I passed your tests, so please, let Ahkai go."

He doesn't answer, but his smirk gets wider, and he scratches his chin. "You're willing to sacrifice yourself for your friend? One heart for another?"

I stare at his chin. "Yes."

At least he won't rip my heart out of my chest, not yet. Not until he gets bored with hearts' desires and decides he wants to continue his bloodthirsty tradition.

So this is how it ends for me. Trapped in a twisted underground amusement park, cursed to be someone's plaything until I die. But at least Ahkai will be safe. I guess this is my destiny, after I narrowly escaped drowning in the ocean last year; I had the chance to enjoy life for ten more months. I close my eyes and accept my fate, but this time, there are no tears.

"What if I want you both to stay here with me?"

My eyes fly open, and I begin to protest.

"Don't I at least get a chance to persuade you?" he says in a whiny voice.

I shake my head and make sure my gaze remains on his chin and not his eyes. But the Heartboy ignores me and flicks his hand. "What about now?"

I open my mouth to refuse him but then notice a shimmer to my right. The basketball court has transformed into a cricket pitch. Does he really think he can tempt me to sacrifice Ahkai for a game of cricket?

Then a woman comes to the crease, dressed in a white polo shirt and pants. She swings her cricket bat and then pulls the white cap from her head, shaking out black curls with blond highlights.

The woman turns to me, and the cricket bat falls from her grasp. She brings a trembling hand to her throat, staring at me with hope and disbelief, as if she's found something precious that she thought had been lost for good. "Is that my sweet Jo?"

My heart skips a beat, and then another, and then pounds so hard I'm afraid it will break through my chest. "Mum?"

CHAPTER 29

Mum's warm voice floods my mind with forgotten memories: her chasing after me at the park, warning me not to go too high on a swing, and standing underneath the monkey bars to catch me in case I fall. The sound of my mummy's voice, full of love and awe, is more beautiful than I could have ever imagined.

"It's my baby girl," Mum whispers, and takes a step toward me.

I'm still rooted to the spot. Everything feels too heavy to move, my feet, my arms, and, most of all, my heart. My eyes rove over her body, trying to commit everything to memory. The smooth light-brown tone of her skin, the way her mouth twitches when she's excited . . .

the way she tucks her curly hair behind her ear! I do that too! And we have the same flat nose and cheeky grin.

My voice inside screams that she isn't real, that she's just one of the Heartboy's illusions, but in this moment, I don't care. In my mind, I'm no longer in the Heartman's lair; I'm in heaven. When Mum spreads her arms, I race toward her and throw myself into the hug I've been craving since she died and my world fell apart.

"I'm so so proud of you." Mum speaks softly into my hair and kisses my ear. Her curls fall against my forehead. I bury my face in her shirt; she smells like the hibiscus bush and all my favorite spices combined. My face is drowning in tears. I sniffle as snot runs out my nose.

Mum pulls away and wipes my nose with her sleeve. "Look at how much you've grown! So tall. You must be a fantastic bowler."

I still can't speak, so I just nod.

"Want to play a game?" She moves to the crease and picks up the cricket bat, her eyes lit with excitement. I bet that's how I look at the start of every cricket match.

She's not real! The voice shouts again, but I dash it away. I desperately want to bowl just one over to my mum so she can see my skills. Would six balls really hurt?

Yes! The Josephine inside refuses to be quiet. I put

my face in my hands in despair. It's true; one over would not be enough; if I start to play cricket with my mum, I won't ever want to stop.

I start to heave, barely able to force the refusal out as tears stream down my cheeks. "I'm sorry, Mum. I love you."

Mum's face drops in disappointment. "Well, are you hungry?" Her eyes light up again. "I can make you some soup, with lots of dumplings. Or we can have pancakes."

I imagine me and Mum making pancakes together and suddenly, the word "yes" is on the tip of my tongue. Would she sing reggae music like Daddy? What's her favorite kind of music? I never thought to ask Daddy before, and now I am desperate to know. Daddy always says his food is nothing compared to Mum's. Maybe she had a special ingredient that she hid, even from him. I bet she would share the secret with me.

This is my chance to experience the moments with Mum that I've been cheated out of. The conversations we never got to have. The packed lunches I never got to taste. This is an opportunity to recapture our mother-daughter bond that was cut short way too soon . . . and all I have to do is sacrifice my best friend.

The price is way too high.

This is torture; I wouldn't wish this heartache on my worst enemy.

I turn to the Heartboy, who looks as if he's seconds away from drooling. "Please," I beg him. I gather the mental strength to reject his offer again. Seeing Mum hurts, but not seeing her will hurt even more.

"You have everything you need, right here, Josephine," the Heartboy whispers, the greedy expression stark on his face. "Your friends, your family." He flicks his hand again.

"Joanne, is that you?!"

"Vincent!"

I close my eyes again. "Oh God, no." I don't want to look, but how can I not witness this reunion? I've often wondered what it would be like if Mum and Dad got to see each other again. Mummy and Daddy. I've dreamed of having both my parents in my life for as long as I can remember. Now here's a chance to see them interact together in real life.

This is not real life, the voice reminds me. I know, but it can't hurt to watch them for just a little bit longer. Just one more minute.

Daddy looks much younger, with no gray hairs at all. He lifts Mum in the air and wheels her around. She throws back her head and laughs—I finally get to hear her wheezy guffaw. It's as adorable as Dad described. She looks just like the image in the picture we had in the living room. I capture the image in my mind to store in my heart.

"Bean!" Dad exclaims. "It's a miracle! We're a family again."

"We're already a family." The words slip from my mouth without hesitation, and suddenly, I see the scene for the illusion that it is. Daddy and I both miss Mum and wish she was still in our lives, but we still have each other. No matter what, Daddy will always love and support me, and that doesn't change because it's now two of us and not three. And I'm lucky enough to have people in my life who are now as precious as blood family: Miss Alleyne, Miss Mo, and Ahkai. They'd all do everything in their power to protect me, just like I would for them.

The thought gives me enough strength to wrench my eyes from my parents. I wipe the tears away with the back of my hand and turn to the Heartboy.

"Let Ahkai go, now," I demand, growing angry. "Why don't you conjure up your own heart's desire and leave everyone alone?"

The Heartboy's face falls, and there's a crack in his confident demeanor. "I can't summon what I don't have," he says, touching his chest. For the first time, he looks like a sad, lonely little boy. But the moment passes quickly. He remembers himself and then sneers at me.

He flicks his hand again, and the shimmer behind me dissipates. Mum is gone. My nose starts to burn but I push the feeling away again. I'll let all my heartache out when Ahkai is safe.

"Sunrise is in nine minutes," the Heartboy says, climbing back into his bumper car. "None of you can leave anyway."

"But, but, you said you would let Ahkai go if I sacrificed myself!"

The Heartboy giggles. "Did I?"

I pause. He's never made any promises.

"You finally understand, right?" the Heartboy says. "I can do what I want. Traditions change. I don't prefer to rip out hearts, but I will if I have to. Depends on my mood." He lowers his head close to the steering wheel, as if he's about to press on the gas. "Do you want to know what mood I'm in right now, Josephine?"

The steel donkey, which had been lying quietly beside the car, grunts and gets to his feet, the chain dragging along the floor. *Reeeeeeeekkkkkkkkk.*

I scan the room again, panic rising. Ahkai is still reading in his bubble. Casper and his wife are feeding the cubs. There's no clear exit. I don't even know if there's another key; everything in this room doesn't belong.

The Heartboy smiles. "You can make your stay here comfortable or painful. Say the word, and I'll bring your mother back and you can stay with her forever."

"Don't do it, Jo!"

I recognize the voice, but it can't be. My mind has to be playing tricks on me, because it's not possible . . .

A black line comes through the wax waterfall and then turns to face us.

"Lynne?" I squeal. I can't believe the sight before me. I'm in an underground lair where the Heartman, who looks like a nine-year-old boy, can summon dead people and control a fire-breathing donkey, and it is *still* the strangest image ever.

Lynne is as flat as a postcard, her tiny nose and lips squashed onto her face. Then her lips and nose pop out like a chewing gum bubble, and her upper body starts to stretch outward. Her spine shifts from side to side, but now, her legs melt together. The transformation is really happening this time; I hold my breath, waiting to see what type of sea spirit will emerge; a black-and-gold snake like Mariss, or will it be a fish bottom?

Her blue-spotted lower half keeps growing thinner

and thinner, until the end of her tail is no bigger than a piece of rope. A white bone-like claw juts out near the bottom. It's only when the collars on her sailor dress take on a life of their own, curve upward and flutter around her shoulders that I recognize it.

"A stingray." I point at her barb.

Lynne is still gaping down at herself.

"Lynne, your lower half is a stingray!"

"Congrats, she's a scavenger." The Heartboy claps his hands slowly and then rolls his eyes. "I'm tired of you both. Ernest, kill them all."

CHAPTER 30

The steel donkey doesn't waste any time charging at me.

I don't have any more knives or black-eyed peas, but I still have my feet, so I race toward Lynne, hoping her transformation comes with some brilliant new powers that can help us escape this catastrophe.

The ground crumbles under my feet. I lose my balance and just avoid falling into a crack of darkness. The Heartboy cackles in true supervillain style as he continues to break apart the ground with a flick of his wrist, leaving gaping holes around me. Casper and his wife grab as many lion cubs as they can and rush toward the wax waterfall.

I scramble to my feet and leap onto another piece of

lawn. There's no steady ground to run on, not if I don't want to disappear into the middle of the earth. There's no way to be sure if the fractures are real or illusions, but I'm not about to test them.

The steel donkey grunts behind me, his hooves hammering into the ground.

"Jo, duck!"

This time I listen without hesitation. It's a good thing I did. There's a *whoosh* as two flashes of white sail over my head, and then, a howl of pain from the steel donkey. Lynne's sharp barbs have pierced the steel donkey's fiery eyes, sticking from his pupils like jagged bones.

"Ernest!" the Heartboy cries, and rushes over to him.

But the steel donkey is frantic and out of his mind with pain, bucking and trying to shake the barbs from his eyes. Though he's tried to kill me several times, I still feel a flash of pity for the creature. That is, until I have to duck to avoid a stream of fire from his mouth. The steel donkey blows fireballs in every direction, even at the Heartboy, who has to leap out of their burning path.

The air gets heated quickly, smoke rising up around me. A wild fireball heads toward Ahkai in the library.

"No no no no no!" But there's nothing I can do to stop it. I shove my hands in my hair when the fire hits Ahkai, my face twisted in horror.

At first, the fire remains in one spot, blocking his face, though I can still see him flipping pages and scratching Simba's belly. Then the fire expands around the bubble and burns the illusion away, melting away the shelves, the library, the desk, and finally Simba.

Ahkai sits on a brick, his fingers still poised to turn a book that's no longer there. He looks up with a start and takes in the burning lair and the Heartboy chasing the howling steel donkey with a blank expression. His eyes widen when they land on stingray Lynne, who is still on steady ground by the wax waterfall, and then he focuses on me.

Ahkai adjusts the glasses on his face. "Jo, I am ready to go home."

My burst of laughter surprises me. Who knew I had any humor left inside, especially at this moment. But it's either laughter or tears, and if I start crying now I won't be able to stop. My best friend is alive, Lynne is alive, and all we have do is figure out how to get out of a burning underground lair in less than seven minutes.

The steel donkey races around me, the Heartboy still trailing behind him, and traps me in a circle of fire.

"Jo!" Ahkai yells.

"No, Ahkai," I reply, knowing he'll try to help. "Go to Lynne!"

"I'm coming to you," Lynne shouts.

"No!" I inhale a bundle of smoke and then start coughing. "It's too dangerous. Get Ahkai and keep him safe."

The fumes burn my eyes. I squeeze them shut and hide my face in my shirt. The ground shakes again, and I drop to my knees, expecting it to collapse from under my feet. I wonder how long I'll fall before hitting the ground . . . Or maybe I'll just keep falling forever.

"Josephine, take two steps to your right," Lynne calls. "I can see you."

I crack open my eyes a tiny bit, but it's still too smoky to make out anything.

"You have to trust me!"

I do trust her. Funny how quickly things can change. Yesterday I was plotting to trap her in the silk cotton tree, and today I'm willing to put my life in her hands.

I say a quick prayer and follow Lynne's instructions. *One, two, move!* I exhale with relief when my feet meet solid ground.

"Okay, ten steps straight ahead. Quick!"

I grow more and more confident as I listen, though I could do without Casper's commentary: "Oh, that was close!" and "The fire nearly had her there!"

Soon I'm near enough to Lynne that she doesn't need to shout. The smoke gets thinner and thinner, and now I can make out Ahkai, Lynne, Casper, and his wife beaming at me in front of the wax waterfall.

Then a crack appears in front of me, larger than any of the others . . . and getting wider by the second.

"RUN!" everyone shouts.

I sprint toward them and don't slow down, not even when the crack seems too wide for me to clear. I hurl myself into the air, pedaling with my feet, but it's not enough. I scream when I start to drop, still too far away from the ledge.

Two hands stop my fall—one smooth but firm grip and the other as rough as sandpaper. I raise my head to see Lynne and Ahkai, each grasping one of my hands.

"We got you," they say at the same time and then grin. "Jinx!"

They pull me over the edge, and then the three of us throw our arms around one another. Our very first group hug.

It feels right.

"That was exciting stuff," Casper says, "but we're going to the museum until things cool down here." His wife snuggles into his side.

"Casper, you can't," I protest. "You have to get out of here before sunrise, that's in"—I check my watch—"six minutes, or you won't be able to . . ."

My voice trails away as it hits me that Casper's wife has been trapped in the lair for more than one moon cycle. More than sixty actually.

She won't ever be able to leave.

"Everything I need is here," Casper says, squeezing my shoulder. "Thank you, brave warrior."

"There must be some way," I say, shaking my head.

Maybe the Heartboy can bring her home. Though I doubt he'd do that out of the kindness of his heart. Casper would volunteer himself as a sacrifice, but there's no guarantee the Heartboy won't go back on his word again. Plus, Casper and his wife would lose each other again. I glance across the room. The steel donkey has collapsed in exhaustion. The Heartboy, his velvet robe in tatters, tosses the cloth from his shoulders and huddles over the steel donkey.

"Don't worry about us, we'll be fine," Jennifer says, in her gentle voice. "He'll pout for a few days and then entertain himself."

"Do you know where the exit is?" I ask. "The final key?"

Jennifer points above the Ferris wheel. Without all the distracting lights, you can make out a tiny circle of orange light above. But it must be at least five stories high. "How do we get up there?"

"He rides the steel donkey," Jennifer replies, and then grabs Casper's hand. "That dinner invitation still stands."

Casper's wife is as kooky as he is. It's a match made in heaven . . . or hell, given our location at the moment.

With one last wave, they disappear into the wax, leaving Lynne, Ahkai, and me gaping up at the diminishing orange circle above.

Five minutes 'til sunrise.

I glance at Lynne's collars, flapping in the air though there is no wind. "Any chance you can fly?"

CHAPTER 31

Before Lynne can answer, the Heartboy releases a howl of fury.

He gets to his feet in his black onesie, his eyes blazing red and fire raging from his fingertips. The barbs are gone from the steel donkey's pupils, leaving them pure white, which is somehow much scarier than before. The creature growls and sniffs the air.

"This is all your fault!" the Heartboy screams. He raises his hands, ready to shoot his fire. Ahkai and I yelp and hide behind Lynne.

"Um, I don't think I'm fireproof," she warns.

With that, we bolt toward the waterfall to seek refuge, but something large bursts through the wax, scattering us aside.

Mariss!

I've never been happier to see her.

Her giant black-and-gold snake bottom is almost twice the size as before, as if she leveled up in a new transformation. The blue and green scales on her upper torso glimmer like broken glass, and they cover her entire face, not just her cheeks but also her nose and forehead too. The only part of her that still looks remotely human is her giant blond afro.

Her red eyes focus on the Heartboy, and she pauses for a moment, startled by his youthful appearance. But she gets over the surprise very quickly. If anyone understands that Mariss has no problem attacking children, it's me.

She releases a piercing, high-pitched hiss and two long, curved fangs pop out of her mouth. She twists her snake body toward the Heartboy. "You die today!" she screams.

Mariss lifts her hands in the air, her shoulders shaking from the effort, and a rumbling sound fills the air. Water gushes up from the cracks in the ground and blasts toward the Heartboy and steel donkey. He gapes at her in shock, the tsunami of water about to crush him.

"Auntie M?" Lynne says, in a tiny voice. Who could blame her? I'm pressed against the wall, making myself as small as possible, not wanting to attract any of Mariss's attention when she's in such blind rage.

Mariss turns and spots Lynne. Her eyes go from red to yellow in an instant, and fangs retract into her mouth. "You're alive!"

The scales retreat from her face, and the muddy-green color of her skin drains back to its light-brown tone. Her tidal wave of water loses its power midway and crashes to the ground, but it's still strong enough to sweep the Heartboy and the steel donkey away.

Mariss slithers toward Lynne, her eyes getting wider as she focuses on her stingray bottom.

Lynne fidgets. "I know it's not what you wanted, but I have sharp barbs and—"

She doesn't get to finish her sentence. Mariss grabs her and draws her into a tight hug. Lynne stiffens in surprise but then sinks into her embrace.

"I thought I lost you." Mariss closes her eyes, and a lone tear runs down her cheek.

The last time Mariss looked this vulnerable, I had accidentally tossed her family heirloom into the sea after she saved Daddy from drowning. This time, she almost lost something way more precious. In this moment, even with her snake tail curling in the air, she has never looked more human.

"I hate to interrupt," I say, a bit braver now that monstrous Mariss is gone. "But we have four minutes until we're trapped down here forever." I point up at the circle of light. Hopefully Mariss will be able to carry all of us while she crawls up the walls and out the lair.

"Watch out!" Ahkai shouts, and tackles me. A ball of fire explodes on the wall above my head.

"Why. Are. You. So. Hard. To. Kill?!" The Heartboy throws a fireball after every word. Ahkai and I dive into one of the water-filled cracks to avoid being cooked and swim out of the crossfire.

Mariss twists both hands in the air, and her balls of water collide with the fire, extinguishing the blaze and leaving wisps of smoke behind.

The Heartboy releases another roar of anger and shoots a thick line of flame toward Mariss. She counters it with a burst of water, and the two elements meet in the middle, creating a standoff: fire versus water, a battle of will and strength.

But after having to fight the murder hornets and summon water from the earth, Mariss is tired. The fire forces her backward a few inches before she curves her tail and uses the force to push herself forward again.

Lynne inhales and lifts her arms, adding more force to Mariss's stream and regaining the momentum for the sea spirit crew. Now it's the Heartboy who is under pressure.

Ahkai and I pull ourselves onto steady ground. "We should help," he says, squeezing water from his shirt.

But what can I do besides give commentary to the supernatural showdown?

I examine the cave, hoping for steps chiseled into the walls, or even some rope to help us climb to the top of the lair. I'm helpless. There's nothing to do except count the seconds and hope that Mariss and Lynne win this battle with enough time for us to escape.

The sea spirit crew looks promising; their water inching closer and closer to the Heartboy.

Mariss sneers at him. "I knew your father, you know. He was a simple murderer—steal a heart, deliver it, no drama. You would be such a disappointment to him."

There's a flicker of outrage on the Heartboy's face, but then he narrows his eyes at Mariss and giggles.

This can't be good.

"You know a lot about disappointing others, don't you?" The Heartboy replies. Still holding the flame steady, he twists a finger, and a shape materializes behind Mariss.

He seems like a normal, grumpy old man at first glance, until you notice the curved horns on the opposite sides of his head. Vines and leaves intertwine through his long white locs, which sway around his hairy arms. His legs are slim compared to the size of his muscular chest, until I realize they're not human legs at all, but the bottom half of . . . a horse? No, a goat. The cloven hooves are pointed and bent, and it would have looked as if he were on tiptoe if he had toes. I've never met a creature like this in my life, yet he looks oddly familiar.

In his hand is a thick stalk of sugarcane, which he bangs on the ground to get Mariss's attention.

All the blood drains from Mariss's face when she sees him. "Papa?"

And then I recognize him from the illustration in the *Treasure Chest of African and Caribbean Folklore* book. The old man surrounded by animals in the woods.

Papa Bois.

The guardian of the forest. The father of the trees, the forest creatures, and apparently, Mariss.

The Heartboy is up to his tricks again, conjuring loved ones from the past to distract us. And it's working. The fire pushes back against the water, and Lynne lets out a little yelp, but Mariss is too overcome with emotion to notice, just like I was with Mum.

Mariss's face suddenly twists in fury and disgust, and she spits on the ground in front of Papa Bois.

Okay . . . maybe not exactly like I felt with my mother.

"Still hard-ears and disgusting, I see." Papa Bois scowls, sneering at Mariss as if she's no better than a chunk of grime under his long, brown fingernails. "No self-control, that was always your problem."

Mariss snarls. "*You* were my problem! Never listening to what *I* wanted. Caring about *my* feelings."

Papa Bois sucks his teeth and bats a hand at Mariss, like she's an annoying insect. "And look what happened as soon as you got some of that 'freedom' you were begging for. You let a human play you for a fool."

"Auntie M . . ." Lynne says, her voice strained. The Heartboy's fire pushes against the water with more force, taking advantage of the distracted Mariss.

"Mariss! He's messing with your head!" I yell.

But she's too far gone.

Tears stream from Mariss's eyes. "Sixty-two years I was in that tree! For what? Falling for the wrong man?!"

"For being too own way! If you don't hear, yuh gine feel. I put you in that tree for your own good."

My mouth drops open in shock. All this time I assumed a past lover had betrayed Mariss, but her own father trapped her in a tree? I cannot fathom the hurt and betrayal she must be feeling. That someone you trust could carry out such an act . . . I gulp. I almost did the very same thing to Lynne. I make a silent promise; if we get out of here, I'm going to make it up to her by being the most kind, considerate friend in the world.

"I lost almost one hundred acres of forest, all those trees, the birds, the animals..." Papa Bois shakes the sugarcane stalk at Mariss. "All gone because of your foolish ways. Sixty-two years wasn't long enough!"

Mariss's eyes blaze red, and her fangs pop out of her mouth. She launches herself at Papa Bois, and the Heartboy's fire eats up the remaining water. Lynne throws herself to the side to avoid it, and Papa Bois disappears into a wisp of smoke before Mariss can touch him.

Mariss immediately realizes her mistake, twisting in the air to confront the Heartboy again, but it's too late. The Heartboy, cackling in victory, launches a fiery boulder at Mariss.

Both Lynne and I scream when it crashes into Mariss's chest, slamming her into the wall. The boulder drops onto her tail and rolls away, and Mariss crumples onto the floor. Her snake bottom shrinks, and some of the scales on her upper body melt into her skin.

"Auntie!" Lynne slides over to Mariss and covers her body with her disk-shaped fins, protecting her from the next attack. The Heartboy gets ready to launch another fire boulder.

My heart thumps madly in my chest. "Ahkai, we have to do something."

I rack my brain for an operation, any kind of strategy, trying to think about the Heartboy's weaknesses, but nothing comes to mind. I need help. I can't do this alone, and Ahkai is strangely silent.

"Ahkai?" I turn to him, hoping he has a plan. The space behind me is empty. "Ahkai!" I wheel around in panic.

A deep growl from a dark corner of the lair gets my attention. The steel donkey leaps from behind a rock, his eyes still white marbles, with another rider on its back. The rider makes a "whoop whoop" sound, and the steel donkey gallops toward the Heartboy.

It's Ahkai! Wearing the remains of the Heartboy's tattered velvet robe and scratching the steel donkey's ears, even as he holds on for dear life.

"Wh-what?" The Heartboy gapes at the steel donkey. The fiery boulder drops to the ground. "Ernest! That's not me! Ernest! Ern—"

Ernest runs right through him, knocking him aside like a bowling pin. The Heartboy yells as he somersaults into the air and then disappears into one of the cracks in the earth.

Ahkai and his new pet gallop up to me, pausing long enough for me to swing onto the steel donkey's armor.

"What is it with you and dangerous animals?" I yell, trying to hold on as he guides the steel donkey over to Mariss and Lynne. Just to show off, Ahkai tugs on the creature's pointy ears, and the steel donkey rears like a horse at a rodeo as we reach them.

"You are the coolest person I know," Lynne says, beaming at him.

She helps the still unconscious Mariss onto Ernest, and then transforms back into her human form. Ernest growls and sniffs the air, but Ahkai makes a cooing sound and rubs his head to calm him.

"Let's get out of here," I urge, when Lynne settles behind my back. "We only have a minute."

I'm not sure how Ahkai knew to do it, but he pulls Ernest's ears again and leans backward. The steel donkey shoots into the air, toward the circle of light. I grip the donkey's musty sides with my thighs and press my face into Ahkai's back.

"Don't fall off, don't fall off," I repeat under my breath.

But as we get closer to the beam of light, it becomes smaller. This isn't how it's supposed to work. Things are supposed to grow larger in size as you get nearer to them, not smaller.

"The barrier is closing!" I yell.

Then, the steel donkey lurches like it crashed into

an invisible wall, and a force yanks us backward. We barely manage to stay on the armor. I look down, and the Heartboy is below us, his face so twisted it's unrecognizable. He's caught the steel donkey's chain in a fiery lasso and drags us back with all his magical strength. Ernest bucks and rears in the air, frantic and still very confused.

I can't believe it. We made it this far and are still going to be trapped in the Heartman's lair, unable to reach the exit about three feet away.

Ernest bucks again, and this time we can't hold on. Lynne and Ahkai scream as they fall off the steel donkey's back, but not me. I've run out of screams; I've accepted my death. I close my eyes and wait for gravity to finish me off.

Then, something damp and firm wraps itself around my chest. I open my eyes to a black-and-gold pattern.

Mariss has come to our rescue again! She's awake and has somehow managed to wrap me, Lynne, and Ahkai in her snake tail.

She springs against the cave and uses the momentum to propel us all into the air and through the small circle of light, just before it closes.

CHAPTER 32

Two weeks ago, the idea of being wrapped in Mariss's snake body while airborne would have been my greatest nightmare come to life. How things change . . . Now my heart is bursting with happiness.

I can't believe we did it. Together, we made it out of the Heartman's lair.

I inhale the fresh, salty smell of the ocean and enjoy the cool breeze on my skin. The yellow-orange sun shimmers above the horizon, partially hidden by shadowed clouds. At this time of the morning, people at the karaoke bar would be stumbling home from a night of partying with DJ Hypa Tension, bellowing lyrics to wake up the neighborhood.

Then I recognize the view as we start to fall. We're on

top of Coconut Hill, by the silk cotton tree. And about to crash into it!

Now we're all screaming, even Mariss. The muscles in her tail contract as she tries to maneuver to avoid the tree. In seconds, we're going to land on that cursed tree, the weight of our bodies cracking the branches when we hit into them, and possibly releasing an army of skin-shedding soucouyants, la diablesse with cow's feet, and mischievous, faceless douens into Fairy Vale.

Against all odds, Mariss manages to avoid all the branches but one. I wince when we slam into it, the leaves scratching my face. The branch trembles but doesn't break. We roll off the branch and crash to the ground with loud groans.

"Lynne, you okay?" Mariss asks, concerned.

"Ahkai and I are fine, thanks for asking," I groan in reply. I bet she would have left us both in that lair if she thought Lynne would forgive her.

The cursed tree looms above, the muscular branches sway as if they're ready to reach down and grab us. Mariss crawls away from its trunk, as far she can go without dropping off the cliff.

She wraps her arms around her body and shivers. Who can blame her? The tree disturbs me, but it was her prison for more than sixty years.

Then I hear my name in the distance.

"Daddy?"

I get to my feet and spot Daddy and Miss Alleyne racing toward us. Coach Broomes and Jared follow slower behind. I jump up and down, waving at them and screaming his name. Despite his bad knee, Daddy reaches me first and lifts me into his arms. He squeezes me tight, and I lay my head on his shoulder.

I am home.

Then he yanks my face to his. "I tell yuh not to leave the 'ouse! Where 'ave you been?!" he shouts, his forehead creased with worry. He glances behind me, and his eyes fill with alarm when they land on Mariss.

Daddy drops me and whips a machete from out of nowhere, ready to attack.

"Wait! No! Stop!" Ahkai, Lynne, and I jump in front of Mariss to protect her from being filleted. Me, Josephine Cadogan, protecting Mariss. Will wonders never cease? Any normal day, Mariss could have flicked Daddy away with her little finger, but right now she's bruised and exhausted.

But Mariss can't resist taunting him. "Vincey Sweets, still can't keep your hands off me, eh?" she purrs.

I groan and cover my face. Lynne looks like she would happily jump off the cliff.

"I know it was you behind this!" Daddy cries, the machete still raised. He tries to pull me away from Mariss with his other hand.

Miss Alleyne gapes at Mariss's snake body. "How ..."

For once she doesn't have the right words to say. If I had any doubt that Daddy kept the secret about Mariss, it's gone now. Miss Alleyne blinks and shakes her head, trying to come to terms with the Mariss with gorgeous legs, who watched her play volleyball on the beach a year ago, and this Mariss with green and blue scales and a snake bottom.

Then her mama bear and teacher instincts take over. She steps in front of Ahkai to protect him. Then she reaches for Lynne to pull her out of harm's way.

"Nuh-uh, that one is mine." Mariss grows tense, snapping the end of her tail. Miss Alleyne jumps and goes into a boxing stance that would put any street fighter to shame.

"Can everyone just calm down for a second," I say, trying to take charge. "Mariss, can you—" I gesture to her snake bottom, and then point to Jared and Coach Broomes, about to arrive at the top of the hill. "I'm too tired to explain a half woman–half snake to them."

"Someone better explain it to me soon, though," Miss Alleyne demands.

Mariss rolls her eyes but transforms into her human form, luckily in clothing—her favorite white-and-red cotton dress. It hugs her voluptuous form, and the light material leaves little to the imagination.

Coach Broomes definitely appreciates the outfit. Though battered and bruised, as soon as he spots Mariss, he straightens his posture and gives her the pained grimace that is his smile. "Hey, little lady! It's been a while."

If he knew this "little lady" had a snake bottom and fangs a few seconds ago, he'd run away screaming for his wife. Mariss giggles and blows him a kiss.

Jared tries to catch my eye; I know he wants to talk about what happened in the lair, but that's low on my to-do list. I deliberately avoid his gaze, but he inches toward me until our arms touch. A sudden wind blows through the tree and he sneezes.

Mariss's sultry expression disappears as she gazes up the tree. She shivers and hugs her body again.

Daddy finally lowers the machete. "Josephine, tell me what gine on."

He eyes Jared with suspicion. I put some distance between us.

"It was the Heartman and the steel donkey. Well, not the Heartman, his son. He's the kidnapper."

Dad nods, believing me right away, but Miss Alleyne's eyes bulge in disbelief. "The Heartman and steel donkey?"

Miss Alleyne glances at Coach Broomes, as if she's waiting on him to dismiss my wild claims.

"I told you, I don't know what knocked me out, but it didn't seem ... human," he admits. "I wake up underground. I thought I was gine dead."

I can't blame Ma'am for doubting me, but I don't have time to explain the entire story right now. "Mariss, how do we stop him from coming back?"

"Someone cut into the silk cotton tree; we have to find out who," she replies.

Coach Broomes shifts on his feet. "I, erm, I may be able to help with that."

We all turn to Coach Broomes, who pushes his palms in the air in defense. "This foolish tree always setting off Jared's allergies! I just wanted to cut down a few branches." We continue to glare at him. "Stop looking at me so, one hit and the cutlass snap in two. I was more hurt than the tree."

"Coach," Jared chides him.

I shake my head in disgust. Miss Mo constantly preaches about the evil spirits inside the silk cotton tree, and even if Coach Broomes didn't believe the tree was cursed, the government stated it was of national significance and no one was allowed to cut it. "You would have had to pay a big fine or gone to jail if someone saw you."

"But it was nighttime." Coach Broomes has the decency to look embarrassed. "After I cut into it, that's when the, er, kidnapper, attacked me."

"Don't worry about that now," Mariss says, "show me where you hit it."

Coach Broomes points to a low branch near the trunk, but doesn't go any closer and pretends to scrape non-existent mud off his shoes. He's afraid and attempting to hide it.

Mariss's fear is stark on her face though, as she stares up at the tree with worry. Lynne reaches for Mariss's hand, slowly, still getting accustomed to showing affection. She gives Mariss a shy look and then gently pulls her toward the tree.

Dad narrows his eyes, shifting his gaze between Lynne and Mariss. "She's one of Ahkai's cousins, right?"

Ahkai peers around Miss Alleyne's back and raises an eyebrow. I don't want to explain the family tree now, so I hurry after Mariss and Lynne, ignoring Daddy's protests.

Mariss goes on tiptoe to examine the branch, still not touching the tree. The branch is rough and cracked, with mottled green, brown, and black splotches.

"I used to meet him at this spot, you know, my first love," Mariss says, in a soft voice. "Humans destroyed the forest for firewood in the 1930s, so Papa disguised himself as a man and bought as much land as he could. Papa forbade us—your mother and I—from leaving the ocean. He thought humans were the most dangerous creatures on the planet."

"That's what you tell me," Lynne reminds her.

"Because it's true," she scowls, but then looks at me and sighs. "But I shouldn't have stopped you from leaving the cave. As much as you try to avoid it, sometimes you end up being just like your parents."

"What happened with, um, your first love?" I ask, curious.

"Betrayal," Mariss said, giving me a deadpan stare. "I was careless and shared Papa's true identity with my partner. He had a friend who worked in the government, and they were trying to buy some of Papa's land to construct a railway. One night, when I snuck out to meet him, they overpowered me and held me hostage and told Papa he had to give them all his land for my safe return."

"Almost one hundred acres," I whisper, remembering Papa Bois's rage.

"I guess, in a messed-up way, he did care enough to give up all of his land for you," Lynne replies.

"Are you insane?!" I snap at her. "He trapped her in a *tree*. That was cruel!"

"*You* tried to trap me in the same tree!" Lynne snarls, glaring at me.

"And I *said* I was sorry! It's not like I actually went through with it. A better person would forgive me and stop rubbing it in my face!"

"I am not a better person!"

Mariss interrupts our argument with a chuckle and then she starts to laugh. "Your mother and I used to fight like this all the time. She was the good daughter, never disobeyed Papa's orders or left the sea . . . not even to rescue me. She had a fish bottom, you see."

She sighs and then stares at Lynne, just like how Daddy stares at me sometimes when he's searching for Mum in my face.

Mariss gives Lynne a wry smile. "I realize now she defied Papa in her own way. She never left the sea, but that didn't stop her from trying to help everyone from the water, even humans."

"What going on over there?" Dad calls, anxious.

Mariss lifts a finger up in the air and continues to inspect the tree. "Lynne, it's still best you stay off land."

Lynne's head drops into her shoulders like a turtle.

"It's not about you," Mariss reassures her, then to me.

"Josephine, you and Ahkai may accept Lynne, but I can't risk anyone hurting her just because she's . . . different." She looks at Miss Alleyne, who is still on alert and ready to spring into action.

Lynne shrugs and takes on her bored expression, but I know her better now. She's pretending to be okay. Here's a chance for one of my dreams to come true, for my life to go back to what it was before I met Mariss, before Lynne arrived in Fairy Vale.

"Here! This is the crack. A piece of it is missing." Mariss points to a tiny white line in the branch, as big as a piece of thread. "Sean, you sure you didn't cut off any of the tree? You have to return what was taken."

Coach Broomes shakes his head. "I tell you, I do more damage to myself." A sense of dread rises in me. This is like actually trying to find a needle in a haystack . . . *Wait a minute.*

"Coach, how did you hurt yourself exactly?" I ask.

"I didn't mean hurt *hurt*," he replies, looking sheepish. He raises his index finger. "Just a scratch. It only bled a little."

Hope replaces my dread. "Ma'am, can you check his finger for a splinter?"

Miss Alleyne is always prepared. She takes a little

sewing kit from her back pocket and starts to poke his finger with a needle.

"Ow! Not so hard!"

Miss Alleyne sucks her teeth. "Stop being a baby."

Mariss chuckles under her breath. "You know, she's not the worst," she says. "Glad I didn't kill her."

"Found it!"

I nearly weep with relief, but I pull myself together. I can't celebrate . . . not yet, not until the crack is fixed. I never want to see the Heartboy ever again. I think about Casper, still in the lair. I hope he'll be okay, but I truly believe he's in a better place, now that he's reunited with his wife.

A pang goes through me though as I remember Mum, her eyes lit with excitement while holding the cricket bat. Though I'm grateful to have escaped the Heartman's clutches, a tiny part of me still wishes I could spend just one more minute with her. When I reflect on the traumatic experience in the Heartman's lair, the fear, the frustration, and the panic, at least that memory of Mum will bring a little bit of joy. I know it wasn't really her, but that moment was real for me.

Everyone joins us at the tree. Mariss guides Coach Broomes's finger, with the splinter and a small drop of blood, to the branch. We watch as the branch soaks up the blood like a sponge, and then the splinter melts into the tree.

Mariss releases her breath. "It's done."

That's when I let the tears fall. They flow down my cheeks, dripping onto the collar of my shirt. Miss Alleyne comes behind me, and I lean against her side.

"Let's go home," she says. "You can explain everything there. We should get out of here before Mr. Atkins catches us breaking curfew."

Mariss, Lynne, and I burst into laughter.

"What's so funny?" Miss Alleyne asks.

But that only makes us laugh harder. Ahkai is clueless too, but he beams at me and Lynne and gives us his nod of approval.

We all turn away from the silk cotton tree.

"I hope you can visit me," Lynne says to me and Ahkai. "Once things have settled down."

I grab Lynne's hand. "I have a better idea. Dad?"

"Yes, Bean?" He peers down at me, a tired smile on his face.

I pull Lynne forward. "I want you to meet my new friend."

CHAPTER 33

Two months later

I wait for the school bus at the stop in front of the hibiscus bushes. I avoid looking at Ahkai's house, in case I give in to the urge to race inside and beg him to join me at Queen Mary.

Miss Mo wanted to transfer Ahkai to a school closer to home. After his kidnapping, she became way more protective. Good thing our sneaking out days are over, because she probably sleeps outside his bedroom door now. The days after we rescued him from the Heartboy's lair, Ahkai complained that Miss Mo woke him up several times during the night to make sure he was still alive.

This time, Miss Mo believed us about the Heartman, and we're paying the price. Every week we have to consume a dose of aloe, moringa juice, or whatever concoction she decides is best to ward off evil creatures that week. She, Daddy, Mrs. Edgecombe, Miss Alleyne, and Coach Broomes plan to form some Fairy Vale Supernatural Surveillance committee. And Miss Mo had the nerve to tell me I'm too young to join . . .

Lynne steps out of Miss Mo's house in Lamming Secondary's checkered green-and-white uniform. Even though she faked her "overseas" school papers, she did actually take the Common Entrance Exam to pass to Lamming.

"Don't you dare laugh," Lynne says as she approaches me.

She tugs at the white, starched shirt with plaid epaulets. The one good thing about Queen Mary is its plain blue tunic and shirt. No pleats!

"Why should I laugh? There's nothing funny around here," I reply with a big grin. "By the way, why are you wearing Miss Mo's tablecloth?"

"Shut up, Christophene!" she says, scowling at me. She's been calling me that ever since I stepped on a sea urchin during a beach cleanup and she and Ahkai had to pull the spines from my foot.

Lynne chose to attend Lamming for a year, against Mariss's reservations. She wanted to keep an eye on Ahkai to make sure he's okay.

"He tamed a whole steel donkey!" I had told her. "I think he'll be fine with regular kids."

To my surprise, Miss Mo was fully on board with the plan. I thought she would freak out when she learned the truth about Lynne, but in her eyes, Lynne is Ahkai's personal supernatural bodyguard.

"Vincent made pancakes this morning?" she asks, peering through the kitchen window. "I had breakfast, but I'm still hungry."

"He left a stack for you on the counter."

"Yes!" Lynne pumps a fist.

Daddy and Lynne connected over their love of food. Also because she found *Joanne* and returned her to shore. Turns out he's okay with me having a sea spirit as a friend, once she promised not to bring her "Auntie M" along on her visits or attempt to put us under any spells.

Miss Alleyne was big mad at Dad for not telling her the truth about Mariss. It took a few weeks for her to forgive him. Ahkai had to beg me not to intervene; I was planning several operations to get them to reconcile.

"Is Mariss still upset about you going to school?" I ask.

"Nah, she's good now."

"You sure? Maybe you should check the cave for any abducted Lamming teachers."

We both chuckle at that. Mariss freed Mr. Atkins

from the cave, and get this: he returned several times on his own! I suspect something is going on between him and Mariss, but Lynne refuses to acknowledge it. She claims he's just visiting the lionfish.

"I have a gift for you," Lynne says, reaching into her backpack.

"What? Changed your mind and want to come to Queen Mary with me instead?" I reply, only half-joking.

Lynne gives me a brown envelope.

"What's this? A love letter?" I reach inside and gasp when I pull out the frame.

It's the photo of Mum.

I run a finger over her laughing face and then bring it to my chest, trying to hold back my tears. I told Daddy everything that happened in the lair, but I left out my encounter with Mum. I want to hold that memory close and treasure it, like our own special secret.

"Auntie M may have found my father," Lynne says softly. "I don't know how the reunion will go . . . but I know how important family is."

I wrench my gaze away from the photograph and thank her in our special way. "I hope you don't want a hug now," I reply.

Lynne shoves me and then goes for her pancakes. "Have a good day at school, Christophene."

I check the time. The bus should be here any minute.

Crackling static comes from my backpack. "This is Alpha Mike Alpha Mike Alpha Mike . . ." I smile and get the walkie-talkie, and wait for Ahkai to finish repeating his code name five times. "Look up. Over."

Ahkai waves at me from his window, with Inkblot around his shoulders. "Your bus will arrive in ten point two seconds. Nine point six seconds. Eight—"

I turn off the walkie-talkie and return his wave. Then I take a deep breath when the electric blue-and-yellow Transport Board bus appears. I've been putting on a brave face, but I admit, I was more worried about myself than Ahkai. I've never cared about making friends before, and I don't know how. The whole idea makes me break out in hives.

There are only a handful of other Queen Mary students inside. Most of the students are probably too rich to catch the bus. I bet they wouldn't even know how to ring the bell.

Stop it! I command my brain. *Don't be judgmental.*

I stare down at my backpack, wishing I had swallowed my pride and begged Lynne to come with me.

Someone sits next to me. "You good, Josephine?"

I jerk, not expecting to hear my name. Beside me is one of the members of the cricket team, the substitute boy with the flattop. He had made a brilliant catch that helped make Fairy Vale the champions of the youth cricket competition. The bus turns a sharp corner, and the boy and I have to hold on to seats in front as it swerves.

Then, there's an awkward silence between us.

I clear my throat. "Hey . . . Adam."

He is shocked that I know his name. To be honest, I'm surprised I remembered it as well. *Just be nice.*

"That was a really awesome catch, during the Pickletons game."

"It was, wasn't it?" Adam beams at me, and then starts to rattle on about his favorite cricket fielding moments. It's not long before I join in with my own, and we have such a hearty debate about who is the best bowler, that I don't realize the bus became packed to the brim with students, until we arrive at Queen Mary College.

I gather my backpack and peer out the window. It's a complex of large buildings which look like they just got a fresh layer of paint. Students trickle in through the open gates, but beyond that, there's a large cricket field with huge lights. I will be able to play cricket at night!

"You ready?" Adam asks, waiting for me.

I smile and tuck a braid behind my ear. "I think I am."

Acknowledgments

Josephine Against the Sea was originally meant to be a stand-alone, but ideas for Josephine's character growth and more mythology and adventures kept popping into my head. I couldn't have ventured back into the world of Fairy Vale without the following people:

* My awesome agent, Marietta Zacker, who encourages me to write whatever I want. It's a privilege to have such an incredible champion for all my stories. Thank you to the entire Gallt & Zacker team.

* My editor Mallory Kass, who has magical powers—no one can convince me otherwise. Her ability to encourage, ask the right questions, and transform my scattered thoughts into the best possible story is right up there with Miss Alleyne's sensei sixth sense abilities.

* The entire Scholastic team, who have been huge supporters from the beginning. I'm grateful to have extremely kind and cool people like Lizette Serrano, Maisha Johnson, Emily Heddleson, Sabrina Montinegro, Rachel Feld, Katie Dutton, Patricia Vaughan, Jarad Waxman, Jackie Rubin, Janell Harris, Jalen Garcia-Hall, Meredith Wardell, and David Levithan on my team.

* Stephanie Yang and Ejiwa "Edge" Ebenebe, for bringing Josephine, Ahkai, and the Heartman to life with their stunning art design and illustration.

* My brainstorming gurus, Avione Lee, Gina Aimey-Moss, and Lisa Springer, who put up with endless voice notes and long conversations, trying to figure out plot holes. I appreciate y'all so much. Special shout-out to Kamilah Hutson and Vaneisha Cadogan for their insider teacher knowledge.

* Kelsia Kellman, whose comprehensive thesis, "The Heartman: The Impact of Its Evolution on the Barbadian Cultural Landscape" was so helpful during the research phase. Thank you for your analysis of Bajan folklore.

* The cheerleaders, Lloyda Garrett, Liesl Harewood, Malissa Elease, Danielle Dottin, Deirdre Dottin, Adn Scott, Akeeba Bourne, Shelly Seecharan, Ramona Grandison, Ayesha Gibson-Gill, Melissa Goddard, Alex Grogan, Nalani Walcott, Negus Walcott, Nicole D. Collier, Chrystal D. Giles, Sharma Taylor, Alexia Tolas, Ellen Stumbo, and Allison Carvalho.

* My husband, Gibbs, my biggest supporter. If he reads only one book a year, I can guarantee it will be mine.

* YOU, the readers—the kids who sent emails, messages, and cards and created art, the librarians and booksellers who got my books into their hands, and everyone who took the time to tell me they loved Josephine—thank you SO MUCH. This book would not exist without you.

About the Author

Shakirah Bourne is a Bajan author and filmmaker born and based in Barbados. She once shot a movie scene in a cave with bats during an earthquake but is too scared to watch horror movies. She enjoys exploring old graveyards, daydreaming, and eating mangoes. Learn more at shakirahbourne.com.